The Crossing

Also by Christopher Keane:

LYNDA
THE TOUR
THE MAXIMUS ZONE
THE HUNTER
THE HEIR

The Crossing

by
CHRISTOPHER KEANE

ARBOR HOUSE

New York

Library of Congress Catalogue Card Number: 77-93004

ISBN: 0-87795-187-X

Manufactured in the United States of America

for my father . . . who lived it

ACKNOWLEDGMENTS

My father, Jack Keane, has a photographic memory with an acute eye so able to capture the detailed past that he was able to reconstruct the story herein with uncanny precision. My greatest of thanks goes to him.

Enormous gratitude goes to my friend and agent, Gary Cosay, and to Marsha Massa and Peggy Jenkins for their invaluable editorial contributions.

Introduction

THE STORY IS TRUE.

At Potsdam the treaty was signed ending World War II. Japan was on the verge of defeat. Harry Truman had become President of the United States, following the death of Franklin D. Roosevelt in February of 1945. Americans had suffered the ban on tires and radios and were now beginning to enjoy post-war luxuries. Bing Crosby was voted the nation's favorite crooner. Hitler was dead, though part of his legacy lay in Dachau, Auchwitz, Buchenwald. Patton rode the streets of Boston in an open car, showered by millions of tons of confetti. Women cried. And laughed. Johnny was coming home.

1945.

The year of the Crossing.

The Crossing

Prologue

OVER SPAIN — AUGUST 8, 1945

THE SINGLE PASSENGER aboard the bullet-riddled Royal
Air Force transport was a tall, elegant gentleman in his
mid-fifties sporting a handlebar mustache and a mane of
silver hair that swept back from his high, unlined forehead. He wore a finely tailored suit and waistcoat with a
top hat perched upon his knees, but his most remarkable
feature was his eyes, turned up at the corners and of such
a pale blue they seemed almost white.

The co-pilot announced from the cockpit door that
they would be landing in Gibraltar within an hour. The
gentleman thanked him and returned his attention to the
dark, conical Pyrénées below, folding down toward the
sea.

The man was Sir Bertram Foote, Member of Parlia-
ment, and he was traveling to Gibraltar to meet with his
friend and business associate of the past nine years,
Catherine de Conde.

It was here, in 1936, near the western tip of the
Pyréneés, that the two had first met, introduced by a
denizen of the House of Commons who had invited him
on holiday. Catherine was thirty at the time and so
enchanted Bertram that he could not for the life of him

comprehend what she saw in his short, rotund colleague, since he assumed the two of them were lovers. It turned out that she saw absolutely nothing in the man but the potential for a business deal, that in fact the man was not her lover at all.

If it weren't for a particularly harrowing incident on that first evening, chances were that Sir Bertram and Catherine de Conde would never have joined up together.

Catherine owned a pet ocelot, that large, fiendish South American cat whose sole purpose seemed to be to terrify any human who invaded its territory. The colleague had gotten drunk that evening and later attempted to make love to her, whereupon the ocelot had swooped down and taken a bite out of his hand. The fellow had bade Catherine a less than fond adieu and hastily departed. Bertram stayed, though not as her lover, for he was a firm believer in that old American vulgarity that one does not shit where one eats.

Bertram was interested in making business deals with the beautiful and industrious Catherine, and in the ensuing years they teamed up on schemes to "rectify the Olympian ideal," as Catherine put it, which meant they staged events, some legal, some not.

They brought cockfighting from Spain to France and England, for which they were handsomely rewarded and from which they quickly extricated themselves as the authorities bounded in. They wheedled a Viennese banker out of his money for the purpose of staging an international skiing championship, which they actually did pull off but were unable to repay the poor man for, since he died of a heart attack. In 1943 Sir Bertram provided the German High Command with certain photos and locations of British weaponry, which he was loathe to do, but he had no alternative. In return for the information, the German High Command promised to release Catherine, who had been arrested in the company of the French underground.

They had profited handsomely from the war and, as Sir Bertram saw it, just because the war was now over there was no reason to discontinue the practice. It was to this end that the two of them had decided to meet at Catherine's Gibraltar estate.

No matter how many times Sir Bertram flew into Gibraltar's semi-tropical paradise, the airstrip which terminated at the precipice of a cliff compelled him to pull away from the window and pray that the pilot knew what he was doing. Clutching the seat now, he felt the landing gear drop from the belly and, a few moments later, the wheels touch down on the dirt strip, the plane bumping and sliding to a halt.

Catherine was standing by the strip in an off-white summer outfit and Panama, waving exuberantly, waiting for the dust to settle before approaching the craft.

Sir Bertram responded to the 108-degree temperature by nearly passing out at the top of the stairs. Catherine stood at the foot, a jubilant smile on her deeply tanned face.

"Welcome to the bottom step of hell, darling," she said. "Hurry, I've got the car waiting."

Her manservant, Baez, drove over mustard-colored flats infested by the rotting carcasses of dogs and up through jungle foliage to the entrance of Catherine's Casa de Las Aguilas, the House of Eagles, a two-story castle in starch white, guarded by Georgian pillars and two Dobermans on leashes, their tongues wagging in the heat.

They hurried through the house to the back veranda which stood high on a bluff overlooking the Gibraltar Strait. Thoroughly soaked with perspiration and near victims of heat stroke, they ordered Baez to bring Campari and soda and collapsed in wicker chairs. In moments, they were toasting the great rug of a beach below and the choppy turquoise Mediterranean swirling among the rocks.

After chitchating for a time, Sir Bertram, who had removed his suitcoat and rolled up his sleeves, got down to business.

"I've found the ideal ship on which to hold the game. An American Liberty ship, the *John Logan,* departing Antwerp September five."

Catherine nodded her approval and then in a smoky French vernacular, said, "Now for my end, the players: Private First Class Edward Podberoski. Nickname: Animal. Until last April with a combat engineer battalion, Northern Germany. Since that time he's been in a field hospital in Liège, for no apparent reason other than to amass a huge fortune at the poker table. Extraordinary card player. Profoundly ill-bred. Rough-hewn. Prolix. Scatalogical, that sort. Gives Darwin substantiation."

"He'll play?"

"Oh, yes. Quite eager. Wants to go home to—" Catherine checked her notepad—"Brooklyn, New York. I'll relay the ship's name, date and place of departure to him."

When Catherine found Animal Podberoski, he was lounging in an overstuffed chair in a private room of the field hospital in Liège. He wore slippers and a robe and smoked a big Havana cigar. The attendant who let her in had to first ask Animal's permission. "Yeah, I'll see the broad," he said. "Bring her in."

He was precisely as he had been described to her by other players she had interviewed: gruff, caustic, thoroughly impressed with himself and hairy. He was also, surprisingly, extremely courteous. He ordered the attendants to bring caviar and champagne, and anything else that she wished. His eyes lit up when she told him about the game, and wanted to know every detail, perhaps over dinner? No, she wouldn't be able to stay, asked if he would be willing to participate.

"Is the Pope Catholic?" he said. "You make the arrangements, babe, and I'll be there."

"Good. Next?"

"Michelangelo Santini. Geneva. Eight-zero-four Rue Lavender. Salon player. Excellent reputation among the private sector. Plays almost exclusively against civilian wealth. And by the way, he's OSS."

"OSS? Is that wise?"

"Don't worry about that. However, darling, I would contact Santini personally if I were you. I've made initial queries; he wants to know more. Stop off in Geneva on the way back, would you?"

"Of course."

Catherine had met Michelangelo Santini in a small café on Rue Lavender in Geneva. She had expected a man quite different from the one she met. Santini was small, severe and rather nervous, not at all like an OSS man should act, at least in her estimation. He seemed to be looking everywhere but at her. He asked the same questions a dozen times, never satisfied with her answers. When she congratulated him on his success at the poker table, he replied with, "What do you know, and how did you find out?" She thought he was a bit too manic, even unstable, to play in this game. Nonetheless, she overrode her concern, realizing that high-strung card players are very much a part of the game, and, besides, his mathematical mind was just what the mix needed.

Catherine paused while Bertram jotted down Santini's address, while in the distance a squadron of seagulls soared high above Casa de Las Aguilas. The dark Baez stood behind her, awaiting her instructions.

"Fastidious man, Santini is," Catherine went on. "Plays with a system of some sort. Also . . . let's see—" she turned the page—"he was a professor of mathematics before the war and an art fancier as well . . . thought a bit of culture might be apropos after the artless Podbero-ski."

"Both men are premier card players? After all, this is the championship we're staging, Catherine."

"Bertram, I've spent five months sifting through virtually every player on two continents. What else would you expect?"

"Sorry, dear, just checking."

Catherine went on. "Next, we've got Evan Hubbard the Fourth, Captain, U.S. Army. Stationed, as you'll remember, with the Consul General in Casablanca."

She had reached Captain Hubbard by phone at the U.S. Consulate at Casablanca. She found him charming, overly polite and almost childlike in his enthusiasm at being invited to play. She felt that Hubbard, as the only officer in the game, would add a strong dramatic contrast to the others. Their conversation was short and to the point, which she knew from his reputation was precisely how he played cards.

"Thank you so much for thinking of me," he said to her in perfect French. *"I am very pleased."*

"Yes . . . Hubbard. How are we doing with him?"

Catherine nodded briefly, with a look to Baez, "All set."

"Splendid."

They toasted the acquisition of Captain Evan Hubbard the Fourth.

"Now," Sir Bertram tugged at his handlebar, "I have a surprise for you."

"In the form of?"

"Private Charles Buck. Private Buck is stationed with the APO—that's the Army Post Office—in Manhattan, New York. A young man. Absolutely *phenomenal* card player. Thought perhaps some stateside color might be nice."

Sir Bertram was ecstatic at the notion of importing Pfc. Charlie Buck from the United States. He felt Buck's presence would imbue the game with a sense of "back home." Sir Bertram would have preferred talking to Buck directly, but instead he spoke with his business manager, Major Peter Tat.

After talking to Major Tat, Sir Bertram was ready to strike Pfc. Buck from his list. Tat rattled off percentages, negative costs; he demanded first-class hotel accommodations and a wardrobe.

Sir Bertram changed his mind when Tat mentioned that, as a personnel officer, he could arrange for orders to be cut on any serviceman anywhere in the world. Sir Bertram accepted the Major's generous offer. He did decide, however, that Major Tat would not remain on the ship while Charlie Buck played in the game.

Catherine was visibly upset. "I've already chosen the fourth and fifth players, Bert," she said, drumming her fingernails on the glass-topped table.

"Narrow it down. Who's the better of the two?"

Catherine shook her head. "Difficult. I wish you hadn't brought in this other man."

"Essential for two reasons. Private Buck has a business

manager, a Major Peter Tat, personnel officer, who will expedite shipment orders on our other players as well. He also helped arrange for the Liberty ship."

"All right, then," she said, still with a trace of iritation. "The fifth man . . . Corporal Augie Epstein, a *Stars and Stripes* journalist in Paris . . ."

Catherine had visited Augie Epstein in his Parisian flat in the hills of Montmartre. Seated with him in the midst of hundreds of souvenirs of war he had collected on assignments for Stars and Stripes, *she interviewed him for the game. She left, not giving him a firm offer, however, telling him that she would let him know within the week. She had not made a firm offer because not once during the interview did Augie mention poker. He mentioned everything* but *poker. In fact, it seemed to her that poker was no more or less important than any of the thousand other things that interested him. She was suspicious of that. After leaving, however, she concluded that the very reason, for instance, why Michelangelo Santini had asked so many questions was the same reason that Epstein had asked none at all. They were both cautious men.*

". . . Established his reputation by beating the pants off senior officers from a dozen nations. Very determined fellow. Forthright. In fact, highly decorated for his coverage of the war. Seems to know what he wants. Strong on integrity."

"That's precisely how you describe yourself, Catherine," Bertram said, smiling.

"Quite right. Let's see then . . ." she ticked them off on her long, elegant fingers ". . . we've got Podberoski, Santini in Geneva, this Buck fellow of yours, Captain

Hubbard, and the final man, Epstein. And you've got the ship. Splendid."

"One last thing, Catherine; each of them does have the stakes?"

"Oh, yes. I explained that to them explicitly: one hundred thousand American dollars buy-in *in cash;* they'll be playing winner-take-all for half a million."

"And they realize that our ten percent fee will be promptly collected from the winner when the ship docks in New York?"

"Yes, and they all agreed."

Reclining in satisfaction, Bertram allowed himself a brief look across the magnificence of the straits.

"Think of it, dear," he said. "The biggest poker game in the entire war. Half a million dollars. One winner. Let me ask you something: were you to wager on this, who would your money be on?"

Catherine spent a moment savoring the thought.

"Us."

Chapter One

ANTWERP — SEPTEMBER 4, 1945

EDWARD "ANIMAL" PODBEROSKI had an affinity for chaos. He thrived on clutter, doted on untidiness, openly courted anything that even closely resembled the opposite of an ordered existence. In the words of his buddy, the late Jerry Crews, Animal Podberoski was a loud mess— and that's exactly how he looked: round, hairy, sloppy, straight out of an Ernie Pyle trench.

If Animal had not spent sixty months in the combat engineers, lugging pipes and bodies up and down the muddy hills of Europe, his muscles would have been in postmortem arrest by now. If his mouth had stopped moving long enough for his face to settle, his chin would have more closely resembled a swinging udder. His froggy, bulging eyes had the advantage of sleepy eyelids, which gave him a sultry, devil-may-care guise that worked very well at the poker table.

Ensconced now in a lavishly brocaded suite in Antwerp's finest hotel, The Century, Animal adjusted the

13

tie to his dress uniform, whistling Crosby's *Don't Fence Me In* off-key. Behind him on the bed his B-bag had been torn open, its contents spilling over into every available space: rumpled and balled-up uniforms, dirty socks and underwear, some nudie magazines he'd picked up on the street a couple of hours ago.

The bathroom was a smear of toothpaste and hair in the sink, combs with missing teeth, dogtags caked over with blue soap, and a razor that hadn't seen a fresh blade in weeks. They told him at the desk that water was short, so don't take a bath, which was okay with him since he seldom took one anyway. The disinfected spotlessness of his parents' Brooklyn apartment had given him a permanent aversion to the habit, and spawned in him his passion for clutter.

Animal was not alone in the room. Chirping and hopping around inside the two-foot-high bird cage was his pet canary, Poncho (named after the raincoat he covered her with every night), a creature more precious to him than his own mother. He had found her two years ago half dead in a bombed out cellar outside Grenoble, and until last April, when they had both retired from combat, the bird had saved his life thirteen times. The method she used was so unique it had even made all the papers: THE GOLDEN CANARY, a *Stars and Stripes* headline read.

Poncho had somehow developed a warning device, in the form of a vociferous squawk, which she would let out just seconds before an aerial attack. In fact, it was Animal's best buddy, the late Jerry Crews, who had first spotted her talent. Other outfits down the road offered huge prices for her services, but Animal's invariable response was, "Life is priceless. Find your own fucking bird." Then they tried to steal her. But Animal protected her, from them and from pregnancy ("Will she lay the golden egg?" *Stars and Stripes* had asked), a pregnancy that he was convinced would divide the bird's attention. Now, standing in front of the mirror fixing his tie, he said to her, "Got some hot news for you, baby. I'm going down the street right now to meet a guy who's gonna help make us *real* rich, even though he doesn't know it yet. You're gonna get your gold cage, your ten stud canaries, I'm gonna get his hundred grand to pay for them. Be a good girl, I'll be back tonight."

The man Animal was heading to see was Michelangelo Santini, a member of the competition. When that French broad, Catherine de Conde, had told him Santini would be in the game, he'd known right then her proposal was legit. Animal had never met him, but Santini had the reputation of being the best percentage poker player in Europe.

He wasn't going to see Santini for any friendly chat, however. He had something much more practical in mind —to find out what the guy was all about; how he operated, talked, ate; to locate any weaknesses that could be used against him later in the game. In other words, to psyche him out. And he knew damn well Santini had had the same idea in mind when he'd invited Animal for a drink in the first place.

A small dim café with a piano bar and a female singer's sad, romantic laments. Young lovers whispering over Campari. Drunken lieutenants telling lies. Fashionable women peering over one another's shoulders as they talked. A man reading a newspaper. Every café was the same. Michelangelo Santini had been in them all.

He had chosen an outside table, four deep from the sidewalk, under a green latticework bower. A glass of red wine was on the table beside him as he watched the cavalcade of late-afternoon pedestrians stroll by.

The few of them who returned his stare saw a small, rigid man in his late thirties, finely tailored, wearing a thin, rooftop mustache. Had they looked more closely they would have noticed two chilly, dark, analytical eyes that darted and skipped and seemed to take in everything all at once.

He had already checked his watch, which told him that Podberoski was late, indicating the man was probably disorganized. Was he as disorganized about his poker as he was about his appointments? Probably not. He knew Podberoski's poker reputation well—a regular foot soldier headquartered in field hospitals throughout Europe openly challenging anyone to play cards, Santini had found it quite amusing. He estimated that Podberoski's pay-offs to the medical staff alone must have cost him a fortune—

A voice wailed from the sidewalk. "*Santini!*"

He looked up and there was Podberoski, searching through the tables.

"Santini?"

Santini waved him over, then stood as Animal barreled up and grabbed his hand.

"Hey, it's a real pleasure to meecha. I follow your career, Santini, no shit, you been in—"

Santini used Podberoski's grip to guide him into his chair.

"What would you like to drink?"

"Scotch."

After the waiter had taken the order Animal leaned forward and said, "I mean it, Santini, it's a real pleasure sittin' down eyeball to eyeball like this. You been one of my heroes a long time now."

"I know about you, too, Podberoski."

"No kidding?" Animal figured there was a possibility of that, considering how well he'd played the last six months. "Like what?"

"I hear you've been playing the Sick Circuit."

"The Sick Circuit! Jesus, that name's disgusting. Look, I played hospitals because they happened to be the only legit places I could get my ass out of the field. I done my time out there. You play in them rich-bastard games, I know that. I heard about you one time in Marseilles, you wiped out one of the same guys who's going to be in this game with us. Know who I mean?"

"Captain Evan Hubbard the Fourth."

"That's the one. He plays good poker."

"Better than good, Podberoski. I would venture to say that among us all, Evan Hubbard, at his peak, is the *best*. Although according to a friend of mine, a doctor who ministered to you in Liège, that distinction should belong to you. He said you were both one of his best and worst cures: you won his life savings and at the same time convinced him never to play poker again."

"A small price, Santini. That was McGraw. I took him for eleven grand. Yeah, a real sweet game . . ."

Just after sundown Animal excused himself and stumbled inside to the john. On his way back he paused in the doorway for a second to watch Santini, whose back was to him. Santini was a funny little guy, stiff as fucking board the way he sat there like some goddamn swami. He hadn't liked him that much, for the first half hour or so, hadn't liked the way he talked—two words here, three words there—but after a while he'd turned out all right. Animal didn't usually like guys who were tight and wound up like that because they made him nervous, but with Santini it was different. The guy tried to be friendly, and the fact that Santini had insisted on picking up the tab made it even better. Animal wasn't losing sight of the fact, though, that he still wanted Santini's hundred thou. Okay, the guy was tight. Now, how tight was he really? What spooked him? *Could* he be spooked?

Animal went back to the bar and asked the bartender a question in mutilated French, then yanked up his pants and headed for the table. He'd soon find out.

"You ready to go, Santini?"

"Go? Where?"

"I got a surprise for you."

"What kind of surprise?"

"Don't ask so many fuckin' questions, willya? It's a surprise. Now, c'mon."

So off they went into the light drizzle that had been falling for an hour or so, with Animal bombed on Scotch and screaming for a taxi until one sloshed up beside them. Animal gave the driver an address on Ridder Straat.

In the dim incandescence of the streetlights, Santini noticed out the window that the parks passing by seemed oddly vacant, and then he realized what they were missing: trees and benches, burned by the Belgians for fuel during the German occupation. He watched as row after row of gutted-out buildings paraded before his eyes, some just recently destroyed—even after the Liberation, the Krauts had used Antwerp as a main target.

"By the way, Edward—may I call you Edward?"

"Only my mother calls me Edward. Animal. That's what my friends call me. Call me Animal."

"If you don't mind, I'd rather call you Edward."

"All right, Santini, call me Edward. You and my mother."

"I would also like to know where we are going."

"That's the surprise! We're going to the best whorehouse west of Berlin."

Santini's face registered instant shock, his color fading from pale to ashen. "Uh, no . . . no thank you," he just managed to stammer. "I . . . I'm not interested."

Animal shot a quick look at him. "What're yuh, queer?"

"No. I don't like whorehouses."

"Yeah? You been to a lot of whorehouses? You must have been, to hate 'em so much. What was it, bad broads? The clap? What?"

"None of those."

"You don't like to pay for it, that it?"

"No."

"What, then?"

"I just—"

The taxi slowed down and pulled over to the curb.

"All right, Santini," Animal said. "You got a choice. Take the cab back or go along for the ride. You don't have to get laid. The best whorehouse west of Berlin ain't gonna *make* you get laid, which is *why* it's the best, you understand?"

"Of course."

But the idea of going to a whorehouse was repulsive to him; there was no art in a whorehouse, just artifice, fleshy, vulgar artifice without redemption of any kind. The profession of whores was vulgar enough without having to visit their lair—and that's how he thought of whorehouses, as lairs reeking with sweaty passion, purposeless, like a swathe of rust on a dirty canvas. Yet here he was with Podberoski, against whom he would be playing tomorrow. His purpose tonight was not to have fun but to research this man, his opponent. He resigned himself to his fate.

"I was being argumentative, Edward," he said. "Of course I'll join you."

"Attaboy, let's go."

They paid the driver off and stepped into what had now become flood conditions. Striding up to a door,

Animal knocked and a peephole opened on a green eye peering out at them.

"*Oui?*" a voice purred.

"Uh, Jerry Crews sent me," Animal said, wondering why in the hell he'd used Crews's name. The guy was dead.

"Ahhh! Jerr-y," she said. "Come in."

Animal looked sideways at Santini. "Ahhh, Jerr-y. Ahh, Je-sus. Ahh, Hit-ler. Business must be slow."

The door opened to reveal a squat, stubby woman with a cone of red hair piled on top of her head, a painted face and a black lace dress that flowed around her down to the floor.

"*Monsieur et monsieur,*" she said, bowing to them. "*Entrez vous.*"

"You speak English, Madame Claude?" Animal asked.

"*Oui,* I speak English."

"So do I," Animal said with a wink. "Heh, a leetle joke."

Madame Claude was less than enthusiastic about Animal's appearance: his close-set eyes, the rain streaming down his hairy face, the rumpled uniform. He looked like a degenerate, which probably meant he didn't have any money. Claude was hesitant to show him her girls, but her apprehension was somewhat tempered by Santini, whose short, slender torso and rigid, mustachioed countenance gave him an air of respectability.

To Animal, Claude said, "You would like to remove your wet clothes? I have robes for you."

"Yeah, I'm for that."

"Follow me, please."

She led them upstairs to a bedroom where she said they could change, the robes were in the closet—"Choose the color you wish"—then she left.

On their way back down, Animal nudged Santini. "Got your wallet with yuh?"

"Yes."

Claude waited at the foot of the stairs, pleased to see that Animal now looked fairly presentable.

"*Messieurs,*" she said, gesturing toward the next room.

They followed her through the archway and into a deep scarlet chamber. "May I introduce my *femmes de guerre,*" she announced with a balletic sweep of the arm. She identified them one by one, and each stepped forward as her name was called.

"One hell of a squad you got here, Claude," Animal said. They were all shapes and sizes—the big blonde, the little redhead, the one with the tits, the shy, hair-over-the-face little girl. Some wore a lot of clothes, some wore almost nothing. None of them looked worn-out.

Santini's lust took another form: dimension and structure. From that point of view the women were magnificent creatures, wonderfully constructed, angular, precise. Divine and profane, all. He could not detest *them,* only what they did.

Claude finished with the introductions and stepped back, offering the men their choices.

"For now . . ." Animal said, head dropping back for a last inspection.

"For now?" Claude asked expectantly.

"Cognac. Bring the bottle." With that he headed for the couch where he fell back against the cushions.

Santini stayed where he was, inspecting them as a mechanic would his machine.

"If I was you, Santini," Animal called out, "I'd take the one on the left, with the tits."

Santini ignored him, letting his eyes roam from one woman to the next until enough time had passed for

Claude, who was beside him, to ask, "Monsieur, you have made your selection?"

"Nothing, thank you," he replied, as if refusing a canapé or a drink, and turned back to Animal whom he joined on the couch.

"I don't blame you," Animal said. "Ain't a whore on earth worth a shit. Automatic, by the numbers, that's how those cunts do it."

Claude cast a disapproving eye at him.

"And you, monsieur, you are ready?"

"I'm working on it," he said.

"Yes, of course," Claude politely explained, "but my *femmes* must be off to their rooms very soon now, you understand."

Animal drew on his cigar and looked over at her.

"What kinda joint you runnin' here, babe? It ain't even midnight."

"At which time I close."

"Like hell!"

"That is the policy, *monsieur.*"

"Then I better get a little action while I can."

Claude waited for Santini to help Animal off the couch and over to where the five remaining women stood.

"Sit down!" Animal told them. "I made my choice. You."

He aimed his finger at the tall Mediterranean type with the colossal breasts.

"Ah, Suzanne." Claude motioned for her to rise, which she did, with an expression of profound anxiety.

"C'mon, Suzy, baby, let's go." He wrapped his arm around her waist and hauled her off in the wrong direction. Claude retrieved them and pointed them toward the stairway.

It could have been an hour later—Santini had no

idea, he had fallen asleep—when he was suddenly jolted awake by Animal jabbing him in the chest.

"C'mon, we gotta get outa here."

Santini struggled up. "Our clothes are upstairs."

"No time," Animal insisted, seizing him by the arm and dragging him toward the front entrance. Santini shook him off at the door. "I will not go out in the cold without—"

He was interrupted by a shrill cry from the veranda. It came from Suzanne who was hanging over the railing, trying to disentangle herself from the bedsheet which had apparently been used to tie her up. The other women stumbled drowsily from their rooms to see what the racket was all about.

Suzanne wailed at the top of her lungs, all the time pointing at Animal, who watched her edge perilously close to the staircase where any minute, sheet and all, she might tumble down. Just then a tall, giant blond man rushed out of the downstairs parlor.

"That's the bouncer," Animal said, nudging Santini. "C'mon, this is life or death."

As soon as they hit the street a blast of cold air hit them, piercing their flimsy robes. With the cobblestones stinging their feet, they headed north on Ridder Straat for no reason except there were street lights in that direction. They had only gone a block when they heard the screams behind them.

Animal peeked over his shoulder and saw the bouncer and a half dozen women, including Claude, in hot pursuit.

"What did you *do* in there?" Santini asked.

"The broad was way too old."

By the time they had gone another few blocks they realized they had to make a decision—where to go.

Chances of hopping a cab back to the hotel were out. Trying to find a policeman might mean missing the ship in the morning. The voices behind them grew louder. At one point, Animal suddenly veered into a dark alleyway, and Santini had to haul him out. Late-night strollers who saw the two strange men in bathrobes careening down the street at them bolted into doorways. By now they were numb; the cold and rain had iced them over. Animal threw up twice on the run.

Finally, at a curve in the road, high above the Quai Van Dyke, Santini pulled up.

"Down there," he shouted, pointing to the harbor.

"What about it?"

"The ship we're supposed to meet?"

"Yeah, the *John Logan*."

"Do you know where it's docked?"

They had been racing alongside a high-slatted iron fence that separated the street from a steep hill tumbling down to the wharf area.

"No idea," Animal mumbled. "But let's go. I'm gonna die pretty soon."

They scaled the fence and started down the incline, picking their way with cries of pain and moans of disgust through piles of broken glass, cans, and all sorts of garbage.

Halfway down, Santini looked back and saw the bouncer, silhouetted against a street light, hurl one leg over the fence and start down after them. The thought crossed his mind to lie in wait and ambush him, but he scratched that idea immediately when two more thugs began climbing the fence. "Jesus, come on, Podberoski!"

It took them nearly fifteen minutes to reach the wharf and then Animal had to make a snap decision: "To the right!" Santini shouted, "Go!" and they dashed off along the concrete dock.

They passed French, British, Norwegian and American ships, and a smattering of fishing boats. A half moon barely lit their way. The dock sheds on their right were shut down, their big double doors padlocked for the night. The darkness made it impossible for them to see the name on each ship, so one, then the other, took turns skipping along the elevated wooden strip that paralleled the dock.

"*Barbara Richie!*" Animal shouted, then, "*Der Ober!*"

Up ahead they noticed that Quai Van Dyke came to an abrupt end at a wall, about ten feet high and impossible to scale. They also saw that less than a dozen ships stood between them and the wall.

"*Pierre Sancerre!*" Animal shouted out. "*Patrick Henry!*" By now he was completely sober, out of breath, and panicking.

"*John Logan!* Hold it!" They pulled up and squinted at the name painted on the top side of the hull.

"That's it," Animal panted. "Let's go."

They made a roundhouse left and headed down the boardwalk.

At the gangplank they were met by a tall, anemic merchant seaman with a carbine in his hands.

"Halt! Who goes there?"

"Santini!"

"Podberoski!"

The sentry took one look at their robes and their bloody feet, the sweat glistening off their bodies, and said, "Come back in the morning. Formation's at oh eight hundred."

"Morning's no good," Animal panted, glancing behind him.

"I'm not authorized to let you board."

"Gotta use the john. We're dyin! Can't piss in the street."

The sentry smiled. "I won't tell anyone."

"Okay then," Animal went on, his teeth rattling, "you hear them voices?"

The sentry listened and, yes, he admitted that he did hear voices.

"Them voices are gonna be here in about fifteen seconds. If they find us you got two dead soldiers on your hands."

"I'm sorry, I'm not authorized—"

Animal stepped forward and the sentry raised his weapon.

"What if I punched out a whore and didn't pay her, what then?"

The sentry took two steps down the gangplank and glanced up the boardwalk where he saw the figures of three men emerging from the darkness.

"See what he means?" Santini said.

"Of all the—" the sentry started.

"Be a boy scout and let us on, please!"

The man hesitated just a moment. Santini? Podberoski? Who knew? "All right," he said.

They charged up the gangplank and disappeared behind the canvas railing, crouching low, listening. The voices drew nearer, they heard footsteps approach the gangplank.

"Hey, sailor!" It was Claude. "You have seen two soldiers—short-fat, short-skinny, you see them?"

"Short-fat, short-skinny!" Animal whispered. "That cunt."

"No, I haven't," the sentry said.

"*Americain*, you have not seen them?"

The sentry held his position, the carbine wavering below his beltline. "I saw two men run by and vanish there," he said, pointing to the wall.

"There?" Claude said.

"Yes," he insisted. Then he saw the wall and realized his mistake.

"They flew? Listen, sailor, we come on your ship." Claude began walking toward him.

"Jesus Christ," Animal mumbled. "We gotta do somethin'. First they'll kill that poor sonofabitch, then us."

" 'Fraid you can't do that," the sentry warned her, raising the carbine.

Claude motioned for the others to stop and continued on by herself. Her sultry approach was obviously meant to dazzle the sentry but all it did was make him nervous. She stopped ten yards away.

"You want justice, no? I want the short, fat one who beat up my best girl and did not pay."

Santini looked over at Animal. "You really do that?"

"You woulda, too, the way she looked."

"And you beat her up?"

"No, no, no. The bitch is lyin' through her teeth. I didn't *beat* her up. I *tied* her up."

"Jesus, Edward."

"I know."

"I haven't seen the men," they heard the sentry say.

"Thees great navy teaches you to lie, yes?"

"Sorry, ma'am, I can't let you aboard."

Claude shrugged. "Then you are in trouble, sailor. I have authorities here in the morning to arrest you."

"Sorry."

"Okay, sailor," she said, "I see you at the guillotine."

With that she wheeled around and marched back to her group, wedged through them, down the boardwalk and off into the night.

Animal and Santini stood up behind the railing.

"Hey, thanks a lot!" Animal said. "You saved our ass."

"The captain will hear about this. Bad public relations, not paying prostitutes."

"Prostitutes *are* bad public relations," Animal told him.

"You know what that woman will do—take it out on the next soldier that goes to her house."

"Naw," Animal said, knowing that's exactly what would happen. "You're gonna tell the captain, huh?"

Santini butted in. "You have your duty. I, uh . . ." He pulled a hundred-dollar bill from his wallet. "In appreciation for what you've done for us, I want you to have this."

"A bribe?"

"No, no . . . a *gift,* an offering, to express our thanks for saving our lives. I'm sorry you took it that way," he said, returning the bill to his wallet.

"In that case, I accept."

"Take your wife out on the town when we get back to the States," Santini said, handing him the bill.

"I'm not married."

"Then buy your mother a douche bag—" Animal mumbled.

"Yes," Santini interrupted, "a lovely handbag, what a good idea."

"Thank you, that's nice of you."

When the new watch arrived and took his station, the sentry led them into the hold and showed them where to sleep.

Alone in their hammocks, Animal on top, Santini below, Animal said, his voice metallic, echoing through the hold, "What about our things at the hotel?"

"Bertram Foote will get them for us."

"You're sure?"

"He'll be here tomorrow morning."

"I gotta get Poncho."

"Who?"

"Poncho, my canary."

"Canary? I don't think you'll be able—"

Animal cut him off. "No Poncho, no play. And one more thing," he added. "I don't know about you but I ain't gonna let a guy I never met go after the cash I got back at the hotel."

"I hadn't thought about that . . ."

"We want an armed guard to escort us to and from the hotel. I don't want Claude and her goons coming down on us."

"Absolutely not."

"Foote's gotta say yes, 'cause he needs us. We don't need him."

"Yes, I suppose you're right."

"Fine." Animal yawned and stretched and dropped back on the pillow. "Gunight, Santini."

Animal spent some time trying to get comfortable in the hammock, then, just before going to sleep, took the precaution of wrapping his wallet in the folds of his aviator's scarf. Twice during the night he was awakened by Santini babbling in his sleep. The only thing he could make out of the garbage was a single word: "system."

OVER THE NORTH ATLANTIC —

From the moment the DC-4 Loadmaster took off from LaGuardia, Charlie Buck had been in a deep sleep. His business manager, Major Peter Tat, could understand that; after all, what was it—only Charlie's first time in a plane, his first time over water, the first time he had traveled overseas. The kid must be trying to block out the horror, Tat figured—he was probably too terrified to stay awake.

The Major himself was too nervous to go to sleep. He prowled the single aisle, went to the john a dozen times, and ate three meals, pulling rank on the flight attendant for as much chow as he could get.

Tat glanced over at his sleeping gold mine again.

Sixteen months they had been partners, Charlie winning the money, Tat managing it. It had been a stroke of good fortune, that evening up on Manhattan's West Side, when Tat had discovered the kid, and a stroke of good business sense to have offered him a proposition: in return for twenty percent of Charlie's winnings, the Major would get him into the best games in town.

"But I'm already in the best games, sir," Charlie had told him.

"Ah, but you won't be if I cut orders on you and ship you overseas," Tat explained, the logic of which was immediately apparent to Charlie. As chief personnel officer, Tat had the power to decide who could go and who could stay. For twenty percent all the Major had to do was redline Charlie every time the kid came up for transfer, which meant he drew a simple red line through his name, and that was that. Of course, Tat wanted to uphold his end of the bargain, so besides getting the kid into games he managed his fortune and kept it out of the greedy mitts of hustlers and con artists.

Even after sixteen months, however, Tat was at a loss to explain why Charlie played such phenomenally good poker, or how he happened to draw the cards he needed *all* the time, or how he was able to whip the very best players New York had to offer. Charlie had told Tat about his early training at the card table with his Uncle Dandy and how he had left Miles City, Montana, when he was seventeen for the river games on the Missouri and Mississippi, and how he just couldn't seem to lose, but none of that seemed to explain it. It wasn't until Charlie told him about certain incidents that had happened to him when he was a kid that Tat began to sense there was something unusual, almost frightening, about the boy. It was as if he were charmed, as if he were destined to win, or at least destined not to lose. Charlie told him that the people of Miles City stayed clear of him after a while because they thought he was protected by some demon spirit, a spirit that managed to save Charlie's life in a boating disaster, for instance, when thirty-five were killed and only Charlie was saved. He was a *sole survivor* too many times just to be coincidence. Tat thought it was eerie all right—but just as long as Charlie kept winning he wasn't going to probe too far into it.

At that moment, the DC-4 was four hundred miles from the English Channel and the Major was concerned about the fact that he still had not had the chance to advise Charlie of the strategy he had worked up for him, a strategy he felt the kid dearly needed. These were no amateur card players he'd be up against. No matter how much luck Charlie had, it still wouldn't stand up against these sharpies.

"Charlie," the Major whispered in his ear. "Charlie? Time to get up."

"The chickens," Charlie mumbled.

"What? What chickens?"

"Too tired to feed them. Please, just five more min—"

"Charlie, wake up," the Major said, shaking him.

Charlie's eyes popped open, and for an instant he had no idea where he was, then he heard the roar of the engines.

"Charlie?" he heard a voice say. He rolled his head to the left and saw the Major's anxious, twitching face.

"Charlie?"

"What?"

"Wake up."

"No," he said, cranky with sleep.

"Yes!" The Major shook him harder. "I have something to say to you."

"Go ahead. I can hear yuh."

"No, no, come on. Upsa-daisy, snap out of it. Early to bed, early to rise. Must feed the chickens."

"Chickens?"

"Here," the Major said, producing a cup of coffee, "drink this."

It was dark brown and muddy and had little white specks floating on the surface.

"I don't want that stuff."

"Drink it anyway."

"Can't."

"All right, then," the Major shrugged and drank it himself.

It took Charlie a few moments to heave his body into an upright position.

"Hungry?" the Major asked.

"Thirsty."

"What would you like?"

"Milk. Big glass."

Major Tat called the attendant over and told him to bring three cartons and a glass.

"Sir, I don't think we have a glass."

The Major raised a disdainful eyebrow and the attendant disappeared. He was back a moment later, with the "pilot's own personal cup," he said. Then he skulked back to the galley, wondering how a major and a pfc had managed to requisition a DC-4 all to themselves. The officer had to be a big wheel on his way to some conference . . . but the pfc? The attendant couldn't figure it out. The guy might be an aide, but then why did the Major pamper him like a baby?

Outside the window Charlie watched the propeller rumbling on the wing, as the sky glowed pink from the sunset behind them. The craft rocked and bumped along like a fullback grinding out yardage, and as the Major handed him the milk, half of it spilled on Charlie's lap, and Tat hurriedly whipped out a napkin to wipe it off. Charlie waved him off, telling him not to worry, he'd take care of it.

While Charlie gulped down his milk, the Major watched him carefully, wondering what chance the kid would have against these heavyweight poker players. Charlie knew how to plow a field, skin a bear, catch a trout with his bare hands and ride a kayak down Montana's Cheyenne River. He knew why woodchucks were the smartest critters in the woods, and he *did* know how to play poker. But could he?

"Let's talk strategy," he said.

"Strategy?" Charlie put the cup down. "Can yuh get that fella to bring me some chow?"

"Private!"

The attendant rushed in and took the order.

"Strategy," the Major repeated.

"Don't need any, sir."

"No, no," the Major protested. "Strategy is essential. These players are the best, Charlie, not like our friends in New York. These men are big-time winners. That's what Sir Bertram Foote said, and he knows."

"I'm sure he does, sir, but I been playin' with the best already, like my Uncle Dandy; he coulda whipped any of them New York slickers. You don't get strategy till you meet the fellas you're playin' against."

"Well, there you are then. Caution! That's our strategy. Play it close to the chest."

"Yessir, I will."

"Guard yourself," he told him, gesturing, elated that they were finally planning together. The Major needed a strategy for his own contentment, to feel that he was taking an active part in this contest. That was what a business manager was for, wasn't it? "Look for their weaknesses and exploit them," he continued. "Make them play your game. Use their strength against them."

"That's all well and good, sir, and when I get there I'll do the best I can."

"I'm sure you will, but Charlie—"

"Major," Charlie interrupted patiently, "this strategy and all, it's a mighty good idea, but you have to understand one thing, sir . . . When I sit down at the table—I always get the cards."

Now what could you say to that?

PARIS —

Blocky double desks occupied most of the newsroom's floor space. Green shaded lights hung overhead, and on a stand in one corner was a German M-42 machine gun. Over a bookcase were two signs in bold black letters: IT'S ADOLF NOT ADOLPH and AMMO IS AMMO NOT BULLETS. Tacked on the walls were dozens of clippings, memos and weekly inspection notices, circus-size pictures of beauty queens, last year's calendars and written orders from colonels on what would and would not be printed. Crusty glue pots sat on desks whose tops were littered with reams of newscopy. A blue diaphanous cloudbank of cigarette smoke hung in the dense, stagnant air. Manual typewriters sputtered and clicked, carriages spun and dinged, pages were ripped out and thrown on the floor.

A half dozen deskmen and two copy boys occupied the *Stars and Stripes* newsroom. Behind the glass-enclosed inner office sat Lieutenant Colonel Arthur Peabody, the man in charge, glancing over copy. Occasionally, after reading a story, he would look up and scan the newsroom for the man who had written it, and call him in for reprimands and changes.

"Epstein!" he shouted, and from a desk way back in

the corner a pair of wild brown eyes slid off the page they were reading, with an expression of *What now?*

"Epstein!" the cry came again. Augie slapped the paper on his desk.

"What!"

"Get in here!"

Augie knew the Colonel wouldn't deign to walk from his office, God forbid—the asshole needed a crane to move his flab around—but Augie figured, what the hell, this would be the last time he'd ever have to face the slob.

The Colonel felt the same way. The opportunity to get rid of Corporal Epstein was the best thing that'd happened to him in weeks. Not only could Peabody not tolerate the man, he couldn't even stand to look at him, at the haircut that raked down off his head like a mountain ledge of brown curly flowers, at the small, round ears that wouldn't hold a pencil, at the beak-like nose and the fat lips that snarled at him all the time. The Colonel had tried a number of times to rid himself of Epstein but somebody—Peabody didn't know who—liked Epstein enough to order him to lay off.

Augie walked into the Colonel's office, mumbled, "Yeah?" and took a seat in front of the desk.

Peabody picked up a piece of copy and read aloud, "In Manila, members of MacArthur's staff received, with *icy dignity,* the first envoys of surrender from Japan?"

"Yessir, that's how it reads. I like the emotion you put into it."

"I don't like '*icy dignity.*' "

"Why not?"

"Too novelistic."

"What the hell does that mean?"

"It means change it," Peabody snapped.

"This is a newspaper, Colonel. I'm a newspaperman.

Newspapermen ask questions. I'll repeat the question: Why?"

Peabody rocked back in the chair and folded his hands over his stomach.

"Were you there with MacArthur?" he asked.

"No, were you?"

" 'Icy dignity' is editorializing."

"Correction. Emotionalizing. Think about the words. Dignity: the quality or state of being worthy, honored, or esteemed. Icy: fresh, keen, boreal, piercing, cool as a cucumber. Precisely what the photos showed him to be."

"Kill it."

Augie aimed his thumb toward the outer office. "The sign on your door says you're editor-in-chief, Colonel. You don't like 'icy dignity,' *you* change it."

"That's an order, Epstein!"

Augie had had it. He jumped out of his chair and leaned over the desk.

"Colonel! I got three years on the Chicago *Trib*. I got five years on this paper. You got six months on this paper and eight years handing out underwear in a supply depot. You don't know shit about a newspaper, you never did, you never will—"

"Epstein—"

"Shut up! I got more. The only reason you got this job is because you play golf with General Wainwright. You can't even fucking read." He shook a copy of the paper in the Colonel's face. "You killed this paper, Colonel, you and your atrophied brain. I almost got my ass shot off a hundred times trying to get the story. And you? You pick your nose and play with yourself and try to lay every broad you can pull rank on. Let me tell you, those silver chickens on your shoulder don't mean shit around here. Sit down before you have a heart attack."

The Colonel sat down again, trembling with rage. "I'll have you court-martialed for this, Epstein."

Augie grabbed the phone and dumped it into Peabody's lap.

"Make the call."

Peabody tried dialing, but his hands were out of control.

Augie snatched the receiver from him.

"Before you call anybody, consider this. For five months you've been trying to get me transferred. Do you know why you've failed? I'll tell you. Because I'm a good newspaperman with a lot of good friends who have a lot more clout than your General Wainwright, or anybody else you might know.

"If one of your MPs shows up at my door I'll go quietly, no problem there. And when I get to the stockade I will make one call. And, Colonel, I promise you, within a week you'll be back handing out underwear. Think about all the 'icy dignity' you'll have to conjure up to handle that situation."

Peabody neither moved nor spoke. Instead, he remained tilted back in his seat, mouth agape, eyes nearly closed, weighted down with sweat.

Augie stomped from the small office and spent the next few minutes gathering up his things from his desk, occasionally glancing up. Peabody hadn't budged. Well, fuck Peabody. Augie was too excited anyway—excited, hell! He'd been dancing all over the place—about leaving for Antwerp tonight and playing in the game. Half a million dollars? The chance to play against talent like Santini and Hubbard and that character in the field hospital up in Liège, what was his name, Podberoski? Ever since the De Conde woman had approached him about playing, little else had been on his mind.

His belongings tucked away in a satchel now, he walked through the room and said good-bye to the deskmen. They waved him off with pleasure: at least one of them was escaping.

"Hey, Augie," a guy named Ryan said. "What did Peabody want anyway?"

Augie grinned as he went out the door. "My fucking soul."

NORTH AFRICA —

Captain Evan Hubbard IV had sailed with his father through the Seychelles archipelago and up the Malabar Coast, and sat with him on the smooth black rocks of Hango. His father had introduced him to Churchill and Marshall Petain and Roosevelt and they had dined with Prokofiev and Coco Chanel. His father had enrolled him in his alma mater, the University of Virginia, and arranged for a captain's commission upon graduation. They had ridden together across their vast estate, Mirabelle, in Virginia horse farm country. Major General Evan Hubbard III had also arranged for his son to spend the war here, in Casablanca, in the relative safety of the American Consulate. Hubbard despised the man.

He despised him because his father would never let go, never allow him a life of his own, because he always arranged his assignments and promotions for him, sent staff members down to spy on him, constantly berated him and insisted he was a failure. He despised him because the General wanted his son to be just like him, which was the last thing Hubbard wanted to be. And Hubbard feared his father for those very same reasons. The General was like a coat of lead dragging him down, beating down on him like the desert sun. It was only during the last few weeks that Hubbard had begun to feel that at last he could get out of the General's shadow forever—in the only way he knew how. Financially. Through poker. Tomorrow he would be on his way to Antwerp to play in the biggest game of his life, and if he won to take on an even bigger challenge—the old man himself.

Hubbard gunned his jeep through a pass in the Rif Mountains and hurtled down into the juniper and water-pipe landscape of the Mediterranean valley. His goggles were caked with mud from driving with his head above the windshield; dust had colored his face and hair a deep reddish-orange.

Behind him the Sahara faded into night; a hundred and forty kilometers ahead was Casablanca.

He reached the outskirts of the city by eight and rode the Ibn Tachfine to Rue Barathon, which ran for one block in the northeast sector. His destination was the T'al Rashid Café where he was to meet an Englishman named Teague who had invited him to play poker. Ordinarily, Hubbard passed on games so far from the center of town, but Teague had promised good action and Hubbard felt a tune-up would prepare him for the game tomorrow on the Liberty ship *John Logan*.

He parked the jeep under a street lamp so thieves would think twice about stealing it, and walked inside.

The T'al Rashid was hot and musty and acrid with smoke. A platoon of sweat-stained uniforms stood at the bar facing an Arab who slapped drinks in front of them and exchanged indecipherable obscenities with the rest of his loud, squawking patrons. The large square room was outfitted with pillars, small tables and murals on the walls: pictures of nomads crossing dunes, a man hugging his camel, and of the interior of the T'al Rashid itself.

Hubbard noticed that most of the uniforms were RAF,

both officers and enlisted men. They also noticed him: his immensity at six-five and a hundred ninety-five pounds, the fair, almost effeminate blondness beneath the film of dust. They noticed the agility with which he carried himself to a table, and the massive hand that swallowed up a wine glass. They were aware of something else as well: a subtlety, an elegance, perhaps, that showed itself in the way he sat, smoked, and crossed his legs, the way he casually perused the T'al Rashid, cool and unruffled. Hubbard had what they called presence, as if they'd seen or met him before, or should have—but distant, as smoky as the room itself.

As Hubbard waited, there was a disturbance at the end of the bar, instigated, as far as Hubbard could tell, by a short, mawkish and drunk RAF major, who as senior officer in the place had decided to insult whomever he pleased. Hubbard heard one of the men ask what squadron the Major belonged to but receive no answer; there was no insignia on his uniform.

The agitator moved away from the bar and chose this moment to pick on Hubbard.

"How do, Captain?" The Major smiled.

Hubbard nodded to him and went back to his wine.

"In the bit, are you?"

"I'm fine, thank you, sir."

"You no longer stand in the presence of a senior officer, do you?"

Hubbard gave him a closer inspection. Short, neatly outfitted, a black shoulder strap and belt and a brown holster which seemed to contain a Luger, a fashionable accessory in the RAF.

"I'm asking you a question, Captain."

"Sorry, sir, but in a bar one doesn't normally do that sort of thing."

"In this bar you do, my friend. Up!"

Hubbard stayed where he was.

"Up!"

When Hubbard made no attempt to obey, the Major leaned forward, an effuvium of candied liqueur on his breath, yet with eyes that were surprisingly clear.

"Up!" he bellowed.

"That's not necessary, sir," Hubbard said quietly.

"Re-member your rank, Captain!"

"I am remembering it." This little ferret was getting on his nerves. But it was not exactly the best time to start a fight, not with so many RAF boys in the place who might suddenly decide to exercise national pride.

"Excuse me, Major," he said, "I have to go."

"When . . . I dismiss you!" the Major snapped.

Hubbard pulled a wad of yellow seal dollars from his pocket and deposited three on the table.

"Good night, sir," he said and started out.

He would have already been in the street if the Major hadn't seized him by the arm and spun him around. An evil, drunken scowl was on his face as he released Hubbard and from his shoulder epaulets pulled a pair of gloves, which he slapped across Hubbard's face.

"Choose your weapons, Captain," he demanded. "We have used words and they have failed. Sabres?"

"Look, Major, let's drop it. You've had too much to drink."

"I shall not drop it. I shall not tolerate your impudence. Nor shall I allow you to act the coward. Pistols?"

Hubbard turned and walked out.

"In the back, Captain!" he heard the Major shout. "Is that your preference?"

Hubbard continued into the street—where he noticed his jeep was missing.

He crossed Rue Barathon and stood under the street light, scanning the area for his car. Nowhere in sight. He would have to walk down to Rue de Strasbourg and hope to catch a lift into town. Damn! He'd gone just a few yards when he heard the voice behind him.

"Captain!"

He picked up his stride but soon heard the quick patter of the Major's feet behind him.

"Captain!"

Hubbard felt the urge to whirl around and face the imbecile, but instead kept walking.

Just then he felt a tap on his back. He wheeled around, ready to square off against the man, when he saw the Major's Luger aimed at his chest.

"Major, please put that away."

"You've insulted me! In front of my own men! You were disobedient, disrespectful. You were insubordinate! You are a coward, Captain, for which the penalty is death!"

Hubbard lunged for the revolver and suddenly the gun went off, the explosion roaring down Rue Barathon in a series of diminishing echoes. They both had a grip on the weapon. The Major's finger still wrapped over the trigger, the Luger was pressed between their bodies. Hubbard felt the steel barrel brush his forearm, but in the darkness couldn't make out where it pointed. Gasping, he dropped his head back and, using his superior size, twisted the Major off the curb to the street, ready to throw him down and seize the weapon.

At that instant a second shot exploded from the barrel. The Major's body left the ground as if the shot had driven straight into his jaw; he flew out of Hubbard's grip and crashed to the pavement.

In the street light's dim light Hubbard noticed powder burns on the man's chin, but as he crouched down to help him, the sound of a whistle filled Rue Barathon. His instinct told him to get the hell out of there and, leaping to his feet, he raced off in the direction of Rue de Strasbourg and headed west, expecting the police to intercept him at any second. Over his shoulder he saw soldiers pouring from the T'al Rashid.

A half hour later, out of breath and matted with perspiration, he climbed the narrow staircase to his flat near the Consulate, and hurriedly pulled a packing box over to the window overlooking the street. He hadn't had a chance to think clearly since Rue Barathon and, except for the image of the RAF Major plummeting to the ground and the shot's blinding flash, everything appeared to him in the dreamy half-light of exhaustion.

It took him a few minutes to calm down and unscramble the events. Running away had been the only logical thing to do. If he had stayed there and tried explaining everything to the police he would have been right in the middle of a murder case, and he could hardly have afforded that, not with the poker game beginning day after tomorrow.

And would they have believed him? He hoped the other RAF boys in the café didn't have enough information to nail him. But even if they did it was still self-defense, wasn't it? Would a court-martial board believe that? Who would testify? The RAF pilots, against one of their own officers?

The less said, the better. He would do exactly what he had planned. He would attend the farewell party at the Consulate in the morning, and then tomorrow afternoon be on the flight to Antwerp.

Chapter Two

ANTWERP — SEPTEMBER 5

FROM THE SHORELINE it looked as if the men were abandoning ship. The *John Logan* had not yet cleared the Antwerp harbor and already thousands of objects had sailed overboard: B-bags, gas masks, helmets, weapons, uniforms, boots, mess kits, all of it dumped over the side by two hundred and fifty-seven men who never wanted to see them again, leaving the harbor cluttered with mementos of war. Troops danced together on the decks, barechested, guzzling whiskey, while around them the wounded hobbled on crutches, shrouded in bandages, their limbs buried in the muddy battlefields of Europe.

Up on the three-inch gun platform a group of GIs was holding a contest: Who could get rid of the most money with the most style. One of them sailed a ten-dollar bill into the wind, another bettered him with a twenty, somebody let go of a fifty. Finally, to a chorus of cheers, a hundred-dollar bill stopped the action, and a tall, easygoing Georgian was declared the winner.

"What's the prize?" he wanted to know.

"Asshole of the month. Congratulations. You're it!"

Charlie Buck had climbed the metal ladder to the bridge and was leaning over the railing watching a squadron of seagulls swoop and dive above the ship. Below him, on the main deck, a formation had been called.

Charlie wasn't feeling well; in fact, his stomach had been in an uproar ever since boarding the ship this morning. Something didn't feel right. He had been introduced to the other card players and sat through Sir Bertram Foote's explanation of how he and Catherine de Conde had spent five months searching for the five champions, arranging how and where the game was to be run, and which members of the Merchant Marine crew would be catering to the players' needs. He had let Purser Larry Kettle show him to his quarters and eaten lunch in the officers' mess. But he was uneasy.

Here he was, on a nine-day, three-thousand-mile crossing, on a ship that was so battered and pockmarked he hadn't been surprised to learn that it had just come over from New York with a load of coal. There was very little room to move around, he was at the mercy of an unpredictable sea that could swallow him up in one gulp, and besides all that, the Major was gone. Tat had left the ship with Sir Bertram Foote, and Charlie already missed his nagging.

As he gazed at the thin dark line of the horizon, he felt the wind whipping against his face and the salt stinging his lips and burning his eyes, and then he noticed up above, slowly vanishing in the late afternoon shadows, the range of storm clouds racing toward him through the gunmetal sky. A voice inside warned him that playing in this game, on this ship, had been a bad decision.

Charlie wore a German machine pistol on his hip, given to him by Major Tat as a precaution against anyone getting at his $100,000. Out of nervousness now, he drew the gun out and held it up for inspection. The chambers were loaded. Using his elbow as a brace he swung the barrel around the harbor, picking out a boat here or there, whispering, "Ping!"

A seagull dropped close.

"Ping!"

He fiddled with the leather grips, spit on the barrel and shined the metal on his sleeve, then took aim at another gull, a big white-bellied bird with black wings and silver markings.

Charlie tracked the gull as it tightened its pattern and, spotting a fish, plunged into the sea. Charlie could tell right away that the fish was too big for the bird to handle. The gull flapped and strained and flew laboriously in a small circle twenty feet above the surface, and as a last measure attempted to swallow the fish whole. This didn't work either, and finally, with nothing left to do, the gull dropped the fish back into the sea.

Charlie had the gull in the sights the entire time.

Suddenly the bird sprang out of his pattern and with enormous power soared high above the ship, out of Charlie's range, where it floated, seeming to stare back at him.

"C'mon, darlin'," Charlie muttered. "Let's play hide and seek."

The bird started its descent, feathering from side to side in a kind of loop-the-loop, a flamboyance Charlie appreciated, though at that distance the gull could afford to show off. Wait till it was within range—that's where the real talent would show itself. A second later, the bird swooped in and entered an intricate cruising pattern about three hundred feet directly above the ship. Charlie wrapped his index finger around the trigger and, just as the gull angled sharply away, squeezed off a round.

"Damn you, bird," Charlie mumbled, taking aim again.

The shot was not lost on the troops, though, who stopped what they were doing to see where the shot had come from. Charlie was out of sight of the formation but not from a half dozen Merchant Marine crew members who, the minute they saw what was happening, took off on a dead run with murder in their eyes.

Unaware of the attention, Charlie bolstered himself against the railing and, with the gull still on target, squeezed off a second round. This time the bird scattered all over the sky. A wing shot off its belly and its head snapped all the way back to its tail, the impact of the bullet driving the bird even higher and suspending it in midair before it plunged straight down again, dead in the middle of the formation.

Charlie lowered the barrel and congratulated himself on needing only two shots with an unfamiliar weapon at a moving target. Wondering if anyone had noticed how truly fine his marksmanship was, he looked up just in time to see the half-dozen crew members bearing down on him.

"Fellas, what—!" was all he could get out before they were on him, hurling him to the deck and pounding him with their fists. After the shock wore off, he was able to get a couple of licks in himself, but that was all. Six against one were overwhelming odds and he soon felt himself slipping into unconsciousness. If it weren't for Chief Mate Sam Murphy dragging the bodies off him, he would have spent the rest of the trip recovering from surgery. As it was, his face was a patchwork of bloody lacerations, his right eye had been punched closed and a steady flow of blood and mucus streamed out of his mouth.

Through a haze, he made out Murphy's voice ordering his men back to their stations, and then felt the Chief Mate helping him to his feet.

"Can you talk, soldier?"

Charlie's lips were so swollen he had to push the words slowly out.

"Yessir, I think so."

"You know what you just did?"

"Shot a bird, I don't know."

"That's right." Murphy's loping Bostonian accent became clearer to him. "Albatross, does that mean anything to you?"

"No sir."

"A large sea bird. You know the legend."

"Can't say that I do."

Charlie felt himself slipping back to the deck, so Murphy had to prop his body against the rail.

"You just killed a large sea bird, Private Buck, which means you just invited the devil on this ship."

"What?" Charlie blinked his one good eye at the man.

"After the doc checks you over, I'd suggest you stay clear of my men, because the next time I might not be around to save your hide. Is that clear?"

"Yessir, it is."

The ship's surgeon hurried up with his bag and cleaned the wounds, which, after the blood was wiped away, were not as bad as they looked. Murphy ordered Charlie to his quarters. "If there's any further trouble I'll put a guard on you."

"One thing, Mister Murphy," Charlie said anxiously, "this business of the devil on the ship and all that . . .?"

"That's the legend."

"You . . . believe that?"

"Look, kid, I don't know what I believe . . . All I know is that when something like this happens, it's sure as shit bad luck."

"We *are* going to make it back to New York, aren't we?"

"No way of telling."

". . . no way of telling? You can't do better'n that?"

"Sure can't," the Chief Mate replied as if it were now left up to heaven.

"I'm sure sorry, Mister Murphy," Charlie apologized. "If I knew . . ."

"Yeah, yeah, if you know, if I had a million dollars, if shit were blue—go on, get outa here."

No way of telling? The words stayed with Charlie as he stumbled along the deck and up the ladder to his quarters.

Chapter Three

For THREE DAYS and nights the *John Logan* plunged through high seas and hourly threats of a storm, its battered hull—a football field and a half long—maintaining a steady eleven knots. The troops and the forty-man crew buzzed about the albatross some, but for the crew at least there were more important things to do, such as manning the weather stations. The troops who weren't seasick roamed the decks or slept or dreamed about what was waiting for them back home.

The card players spent most of the first day following Purser Larry Kettle on a tour of the ship, the location of the game saved for last, until, about five in the afternoon, with a great air of drama, Kettle took them forward of the ship and down into the Number 1 hold—a twenty-five by thirty foot room of iron with no ventilation. Animal immediately labeled it The Tomb.

Kettle and his crew had obviously gone to a lot of trouble to renovate the hold: a round wooden table and five chairs had been bolted to the deck, the hammocks had been replaced by elevated metal platforms from which the GIs could view the game. All this gave the hold the feeling of a small, circular arena, a kind of pit, with the table down in the center and the GIs above. Rope cordoned off the playing area, and Kettle told them four armed sentries would be posted at the corners to prevent any of the GIs from getting at the money.

"As your unofficial host," Kettle told them in his slow Kentucky drawl, "I'll try to make things as comfortable as possible for you. I'll have two of my messboys here at all times in case you want something to eat or drink. And I got another crew to straighten up your quarters while you're at the game. You'll take your meals in the officers' mess.

"Now, as ship's purser I'm in charge of the safe, and that's exactly where your money's going after each poker session and where it'll be coming from before the next begins. That's for its safety—and yours." He grinned. "Any questions?"

By eight o'clock the players were seated at the game, surrounded by about a hundred GIs on the metal platforms. Fresh decks of cards were broken out and inspected by the players to see if the seals had been tampered with, and the game decided upon: no-limit five card stud, one round of cards face down, four rounds face up. Betting after each round. Best hand takes the pot. Deal passed from man to man. It would be the only game of the trip, they agreed.

The seating arrangement:

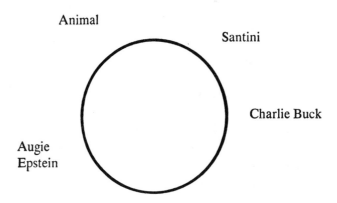

Animal

Santini

Charlie Buck

Augie
Epstein

Captain Evan Hubbard

The first session lasted from eight until four the following morning, most of that time spent trying to adjust to the conditions of the hold and looking for patterns, weaknesses or habits in one another's playing. For eight hours, they all played tight, conservative, close to the bone poker, and consequently very little money changed hands.

Charlie Buck was the first to break out, when they returned later that morning. Buck showed them right away why he was in the game, winning five big pots totaling over eighty thousand dollars during the first three hours, most of it Santini's money.

Santini was starting to act a little odd. Aside from losing, which he took very badly, he started bitching about the conditions; the size of the hold; the pitch and roll of the ship; the twelve hours of exile every day in the hold without fresh air; the weather; the food (which Augie agreed was not good by any stretch of the imagination); then he turned around and screamed at Augie for wearing sunglasses at the table—the glare bothered him, he said. Later, he bitched at Charlie for not calling out the cards properly, and he had a point, the others agreed, though nothing big enough to get upset over. Charlie had his own names for the cards: a Red Spoon was the six of hearts; Apache D, also known as the Indian, was the King of Diamonds; the Jack was Jimmy Jackson, Johnny Jackson, etc., depending upon the suit. It was annoying, but they could live with it.

But Santini wasn't through. He cried about Animal talking too much, and Hubbard not talking loud enough. He blamed everything but his own play, which actually wasn't too bad, considering he was coming up second best most of the time.

Santini's real problem was mental. For some reason, his concentration was shot, the System wasn't working. He caught himself babbling to himself, not only at the table but also up in the fo'c'sle that he shared with Animal. He would suddenly rattle off a string of words that made no sense to anyone, and then catch himself and sink back in his chair, red with embarrassment.

Animal was worried about the little guy; he was becoming less and less like the man who had made the great escape from the Antwerp whorehouse with him. But of course he didn't let that disturb his poker.

The third day of play was a repeat of the second except that now Hubbard started his move. Hubbard played a slow, deliberate game, spinning the cards out of his huge hands, taking as much time as he wanted and paying no attention to Animal and Santini telling him to hurry up. Except for Charlie, he was the only other player ahead.

By the end of the third day Charlie had won the biggest pot yet on a queen-high straight. The hand drove Santini to under $20,000, and hoisted Charlie to $220,000.

By three in the afternoon of the fourth day everyone but Santini had stripped down to T-shirts, loosened their belts and put themselves on a steady ration of salt tablets, the sweat pouring out of them like syrup in the unbearable heat. The hatchcover leading down into the hold was closed against the rain, and the rain hadn't let up since Antwerp, so with the heat and the smoke and the rash of body odors that floated in and out of their nostrils like wisps of gas—and with the boat rocking all over hell—they should have been miserable. Except to feel miserable they would have had to take time out from the game, which they didn't.

The game was really going now.

Animal and Hubbard were in the middle of a hand in which the others had already folded. Animal picked at his beard while glancing across the table at Hubbard's pair of jacks.

"You got a big ass, Cap'n," he smiled, puffing on his cigar and squashing it. "I'll see the last card." He peeled off three thousand and dumped the bills into the center.

Charlie Buck picked up the deck and rapidly dealt the fifth and final card, calling them out: "Four of clubs for Hubbard, and a niner for the Pod. Jacks are still good, Captain."

Hubbard had been watching Animal's face to see whether he had caught anything.

"You heard the Cowboy," Animal barked, "bet the jacks."

"I'm deliberating right now, Podberoski, do you mind?"

With a helpless shrug, Animal said, "Hey, I'd be the last to interrupt your thinking. I got the kings, Hubbard, you wanna bet into them or not?"

"Check."

"Ah, the man checks. Now what does that mean? It means he only has jacks. Interesting." As Animal mumbled this, he stacked $500 bills one by one until he had counted out twenty of them.

"Okay," he said, pushing the pile into the center, "that'll be ten grand to you."

The bet was steep enough for Santini to break out of his depression and actually look to see what was going on, and for Augie Epstein to peer over the rims of his dark glasses. The troops watching the game strained to see how the big man was going to answer.

Next to Santini, Hubbard was the strongest percentage player, so he naturally ran through the statistics on what cards had fallen, what had been folded, how many cards were out. Unlike Santini however, he paid a lot of attention to the opposition, the intimations, the patterns. Podberoski was by far the most difficult player to read.

"Hubbard!" Animal banged the table. "I could have a nap and a sandwich with this. Ten G's, right there. Yes or no, it's very easy."

"I'll buy you an egg-timer. I'm thinking."

"Why are you so slow!"

"Does it bother you?"

Animal didn't feel like answering that, so Hubbard went back to his speculation: Podberoski and his possible kings. Podberoski had invested a very potent element into his game, Hubbard noticed: sound, specifically noise, constant prattle, which intercepted the natural flow of the game like a jamming device. He throttled his opponents, threw them on the defensive and, most dangerous of all, took their mind off their game.

Hubbard saw the result in front of him. He was no more certain that Podberoski had the kings than that he didn't have them. It wasn't worth ten thousand dollars to find out.

"I'm out," he said, folding his cards.

When Animal folded his own, Augie, on his right, leaned over and said, "You're not showing them this time?"

"Why don't you take them fuckin' sunglasses off? You trying to be what'shisname . . . "?

"Frank Costello," said Hubbard.

". . . is that who you're trying to be, Eppy? I got news for you—you're too Jewish to be Frank Costello."

"I have to go to the head," Santini announced and a sentry automatically stood behind his money.

"Again?" Animal said. "Santini, that's the tenth time today."

"What a doll," Augie smiled. "He's counting."

As Santini moped off toward the head everybody, including the soldiers, watched him go.

"Podberoski?" It was Hubbard.

"What?"

"What's wrong with Santini?"

Animal shrugged. "I don't know."

"You ought to," Augie said. "You bunk with him."

"If I knew what was wrong with him I'd tell you. But I'll tell you this—it ain't just because he's losing. After four days with the guy, I know. There's somethin' else goin' on."

"It's just possible that living with you is doing it to him," Augie added. "I wouldn't have survived."

Animal threw his hands up. "What's wrong with you, Epstein? Case of the bad jokes. The guy is ill, you got no compassion? Tough Chicago boy like you got no feelings for the infirm? Some fuckin' newspaperman you are."

Animal turned away from him and addressed Hubbard. "It was nice of you to ask after Santini, Captain, and to tell you the truth I ain't made any moves to ask him about it, but tonight I'm goin' to make a point of it, the upshot of which I will let you know about."

"Thank you."

"You're welcome."

Charlie Buck was sure he knew what was wrong with Santini, and sure the other players knew, too. It was a malady Charlie had witnessed before among card players who relied on strict percentage in their games. Ninety-five percent of the time top percentage players won, while the other five percent went to premier players, the ones who used gut intuition along with percentages. Strict percentage players were like very good big-league ball players, but not like great ones—Williams, Feller, that crowd. Near the top but never at it. Santini had been stung by Charlie's own greatness; his system had broken down in the face of Charlie's playing because Charlie's playing had defied the logic of Santini's system. Charlie knew about all this because Major Tat had explained it to him on another similar occasion.

Whatever the case, Santini was getting murdered, and the chief assassin was Charlie himself. While Santini's stake had plunged to under $20,000, Charlie was hovering just short of the quarter-million-dollar mark, halfway home.

Santini had once tried explaining his strategy to Animal, "Poker is not playing cards, Edward, it's not Freudian analysis of the opponents. It's one thing only: money management."

"But you ain't managing your money worth a shit, Santini," Animal had told him.

"Actually, I am. Otherwise, the way Charlie's been getting the cards, I would have been out a long time ago."

Animal admitted that he had a point—he was playing the same kind of tight game against the cowboy's incredible luck.

Santini hobbled back now, his eyes avoiding everything but his shoe tops, and slid into his seat.

During the next four hours the action was very slow, no more than a few thousand changing hands. At one point Animal removed his shirt, bringing the predictable rash of anti-perspiration jokes from Augie. Once, losing a close hand to Augie, Hubbard actually swore, which, Animal pointed out ("Temper, temper, Captain"), was the first time he'd done such a thing. That seemed to be the high point, though. Finally the game dragged so much that by nine they had agreed to go once more around the horn and quit for the night.

Augie had the final deal. He offered the cut to Hubbard, then dealt the first card down to each player, the second up, calling them out in his raspy Chicagoese: "Podberoski, nine of clubs. Queen for Santini. Another one for Buck. Five of hearts on my right, and for me, the seven of diamonds. Bet the first queen."

Santini's eyes darted around the table, tapping its surface as if it were an adding machine.

"One thousand dollars," he said quickly and eased two $500 bills into the center.

Charlie Buck played cards with one leg draped over the armrest, showing off the tops of his handmade calfskin boots.

"Well, now, Mister Santini—" He smiled, scratching his baby face. "You must got some help under that lady. I'll see it one time." His thousand went in.

"Mister Kettle," Hubbard said to the Purser, stretching his six and a half feet back in his chair, "would you mind bringing me a glass of water?"

While Kettle's messboy hightailed it up the ladder,

Animal, seeing Hubbard set to ponder again, said, "Don't tell me you're gonna wait for the water. Believe me, Captain, that ain't where the answer is."

"I'll call," Hubbard said.

Augie, who was second loser behind Santini with just under $50,000, knew he shouldn't chase Santini's possible queens, but since it was the last hand . . . fuck it, he said to himself, and pushed his thousand in.

"Whadda we got, a little marathon here?" Animal picked up a thousand-dollar bill and kissed it. "I ain't gonna see you for a long time." He tossed the bill in.

"Pot's right." Augie dealt the third card. "Podberoski, a ten, possible straight. A little six, no help. A four for Buck. Pair of fives, Captain. Poker goes up. Two of hearts for me. Bet the fives."

Now Hubbard would find out how strong Santini was.

"Two thousand."

Augie folded. Animal had a flush working so he was forced to stay.

Every eye was on Santini, who knew it, and without throwing out a clue, said, "I'll call your two and raise you two more."

"That's four thousand to you, Buck."

"Right."

Charlie had to figure Santini for the queens; the little guy was playing tight as a fiddle, so there wasn't much chance for a bluff.

"Okay," Charlie said, pushing in the bills, "I'm in."

Besides Charlie, Hubbard was the only player ahead, which helped him to loosen up his play. Had it been earlier in the day he knew he would have dropped at this point, but considering what cards had fallen and the fact he was on a mild streak he decided to take a shot at it, and called the four thousand.

The nagging possibility of a flush. How many times had Animal been nagged by the possibility of a flush? His suit was clubs . . . only one other had fallen, the Cowboy's four. The final decision was actually a cinch—he had to go for it.

"Here we go," Augie said, ready to deal the fourth card. "King for Podberoski, good-bye to you. Santini with a jack, no help. Charlie, pair of fours. Hubbard with the ace of clubs."

"My card," Animal said with disgust.

The hands thus far, excluding the hole cards:

ANIMAL	SANTINI	CHARLIE	HUBBARD
9 clubs	Q hearts	Q spades	5 hearts
10 clubs	6 hearts	4 clubs	5 spades
K hearts	J spades	4 diamonds	A clubs

"Fives are still high, Captain," Augie said.

Figuring Santini for the second queen in the hole and Charlie Buck for the possibility of two pair, Hubbard checked, leaving it up to Animal, who also checked, knowing he didn't have a shot in hell, but checking didn't cost anything.

There was no doubt in Santini's mind that he had a winner; he decided to push the best to get Buck and Hubbard out.

"Five thousand," he said.

Charlie shot a quick glance around the table and peeked at his hole card. Hubbard would most likely drop out in the face of five thousand. Podberoski was through with his busted flush. Santini could only have queens. Charlie had one of his own, which meant that Santini's chances of catching the other queen were remote. Charlie's decision was not whether to bet, but whether to raise. Bottom line, he had only one way to go.

"I'll call your five thousand, Santini," he said.

Santini did a double take and took a closer look at Charlie's cards. As expected, both Hubbard and Animal folded.

Augie dealt the last card, a spade six to Santini and a deuce of clubs to Charlie.

SANTINI	CHARLIE
Q hearts	Q spades
6 hearts	4 clubs
J spades	4 diamonds
6 spades	2 clubs

"Bet the sixes, Santini," Augie said.

Santini quickly calculated: there was $31,000 now in the pot, $10,000 of his own money. Buck had called his last round: called, not raised. That was important. What could he have: queens and fours? Santini had that beat. Or three fours? Which beat him. The only logical move was to pass to the kid, giving him the ball.

"Check to you, Buck."

Charlie made a quick inspection of the pot, then turned to Santini. "How much money you got left, Mister Santini?"

The kiss of death. Santini counted, his hands barely able to finger the bills, they were shaking so much.

"Ten thousand and change," he said in an unsteady voice.

"Then that's what I bet, minus the change. Ten thousand dollars." Charlie eased the cash into the center.

The choice before Santini was a matter of extinction or survival. If he called Charlie's bet and lost, he would be finished. If he folded and let Charlie win, he would still have ten thousand to play with, a measley sum in this game but he had had less in the past and launched a comeback. Of course, if he called the bet and won, he would have—he quickly calculated—close to $50,000.

He knew the only conceivable hand Charlie would beat him with was three fours. Did he have it? It was one of those times when he'd have loved to let someone else make the decision for him. His heartbeat was so loud he could barely hear himself think. His eyes shot like Ping-Pong balls back and forth between his hand and Charlie's.

The final question was whether he would be willing to bet everything on the off-chance that the kid was bluffing. No, he decided, he would not.

"You win, Buck," he mumbled and folded his cards.

Charlie raked in the money.

Before anyone could stop Santini, he lunged for Charlie's cards, trying to turn them over. He had to know!

Charlie grabbed Santini's wrist at the last moment and said, without scolding him, "You have to pay to see the cards, Mister Santini."

Santini nodded and pulled away.

A group of soldiers watching from behind Charlie's shoulder swore they had seen his buried four. Another group swore that he didn't have it. No one would ever know, however, because Charlie was busy burying his cards in the deck.

That took care of the game for that night. Each player wrote his amount of money on two slips of paper, one of which went into Purser Kettle's pouch, the other into their own pockets to double check in the morning. The armed sentries escorted them to the ship's safe and Kettle stowed the cash.

Chapter Four

ANIMAL PODBEROSKI and Michelangelo Santini were the old men in the game. Santini had spent his thirty-seventh birthday two months ago in Geneva, Animal his thirty-fourth wiping out some young punk in a five-stud game in the field hospital at Liège.

When the coins were tossed to divvy up the ship's accommodations the two old men got to share a fo'c'sle together. Augie and Hubbard were next door.

Even then the Cowboy's luck was running—he got the third room to himself.

The quarters had hardly enough room for one man—two bunks with plain steel lockers, a porthole, a bench and a wastebasket, and plywood bulkheads. A sign next to Animal's bunk read: ESCAPE PANEL KICK OUT.

It was nearly one A.M. and Animal had been trying to sleep for an hour, which was nothing new. This was the fourth night in a row for Santini's Mounting Problems. The more money he lost, the longer he stayed awake, so by implication, the problems had also become Animal's since he couldn't sleep with the light on.

Animal realized, though, that it wasn't really the light that was keeping him awake but the noise Santini was making; the scratchings and scribblings he entered into his notebook, the turning of pages, the sighs and the moans, the anguish of a man on the brink of losing his fortune.

Each player carried a notebook of sorts with him, a compilation of attitudes and reminders about the others' methods of play, hints picked up, characteristics, habits to be turned against them later in the game. Santini had one of his own.

Player	*Emotional Characteristics*
CHARLIE BUCK	Child-like when winning. Given to mild temper tantrums when losing a big hand. While others fade at end of day, his stamina accelerates. Fiddles with his belt buckle.
CAPTAIN HUBBARD	Stoic. Hard to read. Plays tight when ahead. Loosens up otherwise. Interesting hands, esp. the fingers. Watch them. There are patterns in them. Inferiority complex. Low confidence behind strong facade.
AUGIE EPSTEIN	Basically sincere. Asks a lot of questions. Relies on giving off phony signals. High tension when losing, very tight.

EDWARD PODBEROSKI   Exterior killer instinct, interior mush. Plays brilliantly sloppy, or so it seems. Talks more with good hands.

Santini's problem was that he spent four or five hours a night at it, jotting down material like this, some valuable but mostly gibberish. (Animal had sneaked a look at a few pages last night and found them full of repetitious nonsense—hardly any of it to do with the game or the players.)

A number of times Animal had been ready to leap out of bed and unleash a torrent of curses at the floundering Santini, in an effort to drive the man away from his asinine System and back into his brain, which is where he'd find a cure if there was one. Santini had become obsessed with lost poker hands. He'd become the consummate second-guesser, replaying old cards like old embarrassments he would never live down.

"Santini?" Animal said from under the covers.

"Yes, Edward?"

"You can't keep doing this."

"Doing what?"

The covers folded away and Animal's hairy skull revealed itself, his small bloodshot eyes half crossed in anger.

"This! The scratchin' on the paper. The light. I know we all gotta make notes on each other. I make mental notes. You write it all down. That's terrific but not at one in the morning. I can't sleep. I can't stay awake. It's one of them either-or situations. Either you turn off the light or I turn it off for you. I ain't a bad guy, but for crissakes . . ."

In a dreamy, monotonous cadence, Santini replied: "You must understand something, Edward. This is the only opportunity I have to make my notations. I apologize for the inconvenience but there is nothing either of us can do, except to embrace the situation and all of its ramifications."

Animal cocked his head with an expression of profound befuddlement. Santini added to the murk with: "Discipline, Edward. Cerebral symmetry. The balance of nature. It's no wonder that along with mathematics I have concentrated my energies on the most structural period in man's recent history—the eighteenth century. Versailles was constructed during that time, Edward, man's perfect gift to his perfect universe. God has been at Versailles."

He then launched into an explanation of the Pope-Leibnitz-Rousseau-Great Chain of Being-Monad-Cause and Effect school, the search for the Grand Plan.

Santini prepared for another philosophical barrage but this time Animal wasn't ready to listen.

"Santini, what the hell's this got to do with your scratchin' around at one in the morning!"

"Rousseau belived that the Lisbon earthquake was caused by too many people living in Lisbon. Their weight did it."

"And this Rousseau was a thinker?" Animal decided to humor him after all: the man was not well.

"Of the most imaginative kind."

"I can believe it."

Santini pinched the St. Christopher medal around his neck. "My mother used to tell me—and I'm convinced she was right—that I am the natural inheritor of the consciousness of these great men's thoughts. In the system of things I am the conduit through which history passes." Santini seemed pleased with that notion and took a moment to reflect upon it.

During the next few minutes Animal listened to him

ramble on about such things as: the sublime, the Catholic Church, *Sturm und Drang,* the struggle of the individual against the world, enlightenment, rationalism, a guy named Locke, another one, Diderot. Who knew? The Salon Carré, Prix de Rome, neoclassicism, Baroque architecture. Santini was on the edge of his bunk now, bombarding him, spewing out history. What history? Whose history? No, Animal thought, this was not the same guy who had made the great escape—

"Hold it!" Animal shouted, squinting into Santini's face. "That's it!"

"That's what?"

"You caught the clap! From one of them broads back at Claude's. I don't know how, but, Jesus Christ, why didn't I see it before? You know what the clap can do to somebody's brain? Look what it's done to yours. We got to get you to the infirmary."

"I did not catch the clap. I was not with any of those women." Santini inhaled deeply and lifted his head in cosmic speculation. "I must sleep now, Edward. Thank you for taking time out to talk with me. I haven't had the opportunity to do that in a very long time. Good night, Edward."

Santini reached up and switched off the lamp, then rolled back into his bunk, pulling the covers with him. Traces of blue light filtered in from the corridor, bathing Animal's face. He neither moved nor spoke nor focused his eyes on anything in particular. Frowning now, he wondered why, after sixty months of running across just about every oddball he could imagine, he was not prepared for the spectacle and weird transformation of Michelangelo Santini.

Whenever Augie Epstein figured he had made a wrong turn somewhere, pulled a boner or simply fucked up, he took it out on himself by joining his middle and index fingers and lacerating a tiny bald spot at the crown of his skull, rubbing it raw and bloody, as if attacking the part of his brain responsible for the fuckup.

This self-immolation was not new, for beneath Augie's ordinary looks was a very unordinary temper. His earliest memory of the temper was at six when one day he demanded a glass of milk from his mother, who told him he would have to wait. Augie refused to wait and instead chewed the glass to bits and spit it out. Whenever he wanted to impress someone with just how temperamental he could be, he opened his mouth and stuck out his tongue to reveal dozens of tiny scars zigzagging over its surface.

This and other forms of aberrant behavior made one thing very clear to Augie—he was capable of anything to get his own way. He worked out a simple equation which he wrote out on the back of his school report card: "Money means winning. Winning means power. Power feels better than anything." He also knew that in order to get money and power he would have to do more than walk around chewing glass in people's faces. Since he wasn't the biggest guy around he had to rely not on physical power but on brain power to make his fortune. He had to be more than smart—he had to be brilliant.

On freezing Chicago winter mornings he sold flowers on street corners. But while the other kids sold bunches for twenty-five cents apiece, Augie sold them for fifty cents. At double the price, his customers figured his bunches must be at least twice as good, which of course they weren't, and with the extra pocket money Augie took the other kids for steak dinners, thus buying their friendship and keeping them off his back in neighborhood business matters.

Augie had another hold over them, too. His single in-

satiable desire then, as now, was to win. And when he
didn't, he threw such fits that the other kids, knowing
how violent he was, often let him win, or so they thought.
The general opinion of their parents was that by the time
Augie was twenty-five, he'd either be a millionaire or a
convict—or dead.

Having lost all their money during the Depression,
Augie's parents decided to make up for it by having six
children—five girls and Augie himself. His sisters pam-
pered him, often did what he asked, and soon found
themselves being roundly manipulated. His mother's
death when he was twelve, which he saw as desertion,
fortified his attitude toward women as soft, malleable
creatures, to be maligned, utilized and taken advantage
of. At the same time, however, he realized their impor-
tance as a means by which to accelerate his career.

His first marriage—at eighteen—was to a girl whose
family owned the largest florist-shop chain in Chicago.
Augie was naturally given his own store and within a
year turned it into the chain's biggest money-maker, at
which point he divorced her. And they kicked him out.

His second marriage—a year later—was to a woman
three years his senior whose family owned a major share
of the *Chicago Tribune,* on which Augie became a reporter. He almost divorced her, too, but to his surprise
found he really liked the job.

Meanwhile, the same kid who had sold flowers for
twice what the other kids offered, the same young man
who had gambled away love for a career, discovered
within him the makings of an excellent card player. From
pitching pennies along Michigan Avenue to throwing
craps down in The Loop, Augie graduated to all-night
poker sessions with his cronies, and by the time he'd
reached twenty, he was leaving the table at dawn with
five, sometimes ten times more than he had invested.

When the war came he used his contacts at the *Trib* to secure a job with *Stars and Stripes*. Writing for *Stars and Stripes* served two purposes: it enabled him to go places and meet people whom he might be able to use later on; and it satisfied his impulse for adventure.

He always volunteered for the paper's most dangerous assignments. Whenever he learned of an invasion or aerial attack—anything that might jeopardize a reporter's life—Augie begged to cover the story, and usually took off whether he got the assignment or not, because he *knew* he could write a better version than anyone else. He carried the same attitude into a poker game: he knew he would leave the table richer.

Which was precisely the reason for his dilemma now, the reason for tearing at his scalp. He was losing, and badly.

He had risen and dressed quietly so as not to wake Hubbard, who was snoring in the opposite bunk, and made his way topside, angling toward the rear of the ship, to the five-inch gun platform. He stood there now, bundled up against the bitter cold gale winds sweeping off the bow. With the sunrise just moments away, the sky the color of an old photograph, Augie watched the trail of foam meandering off toward the horizon and listened as the steering gear groaned below him like a melancholy drunk.

It didn't take him long to realize that losing wasn't the main problem—in fact, it wasn't the game at all. The mistake he'd made was leaving Paris in the first place. He didn't have a goddamn thing to go back to in the States, except for his family, but he'd been away from them so long he hardly ever thought about them. He had made a snap decision to play in this game, which wasn't like him, but then again he hadn't had much time to consider the situation.

What an idiot. He had had it made in Paris, especially since the end of the war. He had had women and dough and any goddamn thing he wanted just by making a phone call. And what better place to operate from than *Stars and Stripes?* He had been wiping out those old military farts at the poker table. He'd lived in a goddamn palace up in Montmartre.

And so what had he done? Been seduced away by a poker game and a shot at winning half a million bucks on this ridiculous piece of scrap iron, and playing cards against the best. That had been the clincher, when the De Conde woman had told him whom he would be playing against. Now, thanks to his goddamn vanity, he was almost a hundred thou in the hole . . .

Augie spent about an hour and a half on deck, bitching and moaning to himself and mulling over all the things he should have done, when suddenly the morning sunlight beating down on his head seemed to clear the fog in his brain. Jesus, what was wrong with him? He felt like kicking himself in the ass. Was this how he had always won—by feeling sorry for himself? You want to win the goddamn game, he told himself, go ahead and win the goddamn game. Take charge. *Do* something.

He would go back to the table and play ferocious fucking poker. Paris wasn't going to move. Nothing was going to move unless he moved himself. Plus picking his scalp was giving him one hell of a headache.

Get back in that game and bust ass. With that message firmly in his mind, he wheeled around and marched back to his room.

During the last four days, Charlie Buck and Evan Hubbard had discovered, strange as it seemed, that they shared other interests besides poker. They both knew horses, for instance, Hubbard chatting about his favorite

Tennessee Walkers, and Charlie going on about his paints and ponies. Charlie really was a Western boy. When Animal had nicknamed him Cowboy, it wasn't just for his Montana twang. Charlie's poker uniform consisted of leather vest, checkered shirt, big, wide buckle, string tie and hat, and pointed, embroidered boots. The uniform was halfway between Doc Holliday and a ranch hand— not too much or too little, just natural—and Charlie donned them each day with the precision of a soldier executing the Manual of Arms.

The two of them were in Charlie's room now, having just come in from breakfast. Sometimes their talk was casual, their meetings accidental, but not this time. Hubbard was here on a mission, with the help of some prodding from Augie.

He was seated on a bare mattress across from Charlie's bunk, bent forward, hands cupped, elbows on his thighs, wondering how he was going to work this. Finally, he said easily, "How's the action back in New York?"

Charlie was busy checking himself out in the mirror.

"Lots of different kinds, Cap'n. How 'bout down where you were?"

"Same sort of thing," Hubbard said. "But relatively weak. A lot of Arab money in Casablanca, and military, but the best it has is a strong amateur class."

"Oh, I played against some big beef in New York, some of them stock-market people. They're like machines, like Santini."

Hubbard crossed his knees in preparation for changing the subject. "That officer that came on board with you, Major Tat? He's your commanding officer?"

"In a manner of speaking."

"In a manner of speaking?"

"Major Tat's my personnel officer, Cap'n, the man in charge of shipping all personnel overseas."

"And what did he arrange with you, Charlie, in terms of being shipped overseas?"

"He's my business manager."

"And what is his association with Sir Bertram Foote and Catherine de Conde?"

"Far as I know, sir, they contacted him when they heard about how I was winning and invited me to play in this game."

"You've been playing very well, Charlie."

"I do my best." Charlie was secretly enjoying Hubbard's questions. It showed the man was unnerved by how much Charlie had won—it'd happened time and time again during his career: Charlie'd been quizzed and cross-examined and interrogated by card players who simply could not believe that a young kid like himself could take them to the cleaners night after night. Which was their problem, not his.

"What other questions would you like to ask me, sir?"

"I'm not just here asking questions, Charlie. I'm interested in finding out certain things."

"Like what?"

"I'm interested in the fact that of the five of us, you are the only one who no one knows a thing about."

"I never heard of any of you either."

"You're the only one *no* one's heard about, Charlie."

Charlie leaned back against the bunk and scratched the side of his head, and then with a smile said, "You know, sir, if I wasn't so easygoing I could take real offense at what you're sugesting here. And I sure as hell ain't gonna start defending myself. Couldn't do that, since there ain't nothing to defend myself against. You know, my Uncle Dandy once told me that a great poker player never had to look at his cards, all he had to do was look at the other fellers' faces, and I'll tell you, I've been looking at all your faces these past four days, and there ain't a winner in the bunch." He flashed his smile again. "No offense, sir."

Hubbard's face froze and he got up abruptly. "Yes, well, we'll just see about that. Just remember, Buck, we'll be keeping an eye on you. . . . See you in The Tomb." He stalked out of the room.

Charlie sat down on the bunk and thought what a kick it was, Hubbard coming in here with his hints and accusations. He knew it was just a tactic to try to throw him off his game. Well, let's see how he liked a bit of his own back. All the fears that had assaulted Charlie that first morning on the boat were gone, now that he saw how the game was going. Whistling, he stood up again to straighten his hat in the mirror. Yes sir, not a winner in the bunch . . .

Chapter Five

RIGHT ON SCHEDULE, Purser Larry Kettle, escorted by two armed sentries, climbed down into the hold with a satchel containing twenty fresh decks of cards and $500,000 in cash. A couple of days ago, he had complained about carrying that much cash back and forth from the ship's safe to the hold and back every day, but Animal had explained to him.

"Me and everybody else at this game plays for cash dollars, Red. I know it ain't safe haulin' the dough from the safe every morning, but who would take it? Where would they go? Atlantis? I like to see the half million bucks on the table. It gives me inspiration."

A few dozen soldiers were lingering outside the Number 1 hatch, a few dozen more than usual because the word was out that a special event would be happening today: Santini's death at the poker table. A lottery had started up as to the exact moment of Santini's demise. Most of the action was on between three and four in the afternoon.

Animal arrived first to hold his daily press conference: "Good morning, you degenerates. Who else but a degenerate would show up here at ten in the morning in this weather? All right, the forecast of the day: Santini makes a comeback."

He heard a few "bullshits!" from the crowd and held up his hands until the noise died. "Hey, this is *my* forecast, take it or leave it, I don't care. I didn't say he was gonna *win*. As far as my own playing's concerned, I can personally inform you I have discovered habits in two of the players that give me a shot at taking it all."

He pulled a cigar from his breast pocket and there was a light waiting for him.

"And one more thing, fellas . . . You been riding the Cowboy pretty hard the last few days. I know he ain't been the war hero you fuckers been, and he shot that damn bird, but ease up, will ya? When I beat him, I intend to beat him *my* way. This ain't no criticism, fellas, I'm just doing a little charity work."

He let that sink in, then, "So like I said, Santini makes a comeback. Hubbard and Eppy take a dive. The Cowboy remains the same. For you day-by-day bettors," he winked, "I recommend me."

He walked over to the table and sat down. Yeah; Santini would make a comeback, he could sense that, but then there was the other half of the prophecy: after the comeback Santini would lose it all, in a hurry. *That* he would have bet on. Animal foresaw more sleepless nights.

The second to arrive was Charlie Buck, who was greeted with markedly less enthusiasm. Animal was right about what he'd said earlier—congenial as he was, Charlie was not a favorite among the troops, who didn't appreciate the idea that he had spent the war in a New York City post office. Going around potting albatrosses didn't help, either. Their chilliness didn't seem to bother Charlie, though, who contented himself with a "Good mornin', nice to see yuh," and took his place.

Hubbard arrived, to be met by a chorus of cracks about what was it like being an officer and losing to a pfc. Hubbard only smiled and sat down. Despite Charlie's streak, the smart money, it was rumored, was riding on Hubbard to win in the end.

Augie showed up last because every morning after breakfast he went back to his room to exercise. He would sit, inhaling and exhaling, visualizing the air traveling through his body to a spot five inches below his navel. This spot, according to a buddy of his who had traveled in the Far East, was the source of all energy. Augie had been doing this exercise for three years now and could restore concentration within a minute, which he thought was pretty damn good for a non-Oriental Jewish kid from Chicago.

By ten-fifteen all the players were present with the exception of Santini. Kettle sent one of his men to look for him.

"The last time I seen Santini was on the john," Animal said. "He coulda fallen in."

"Kettle," Augie began to complain, "you *have* to do something about the smoke in this goddamn place. How do you expect—?"

Suddenly, they heard a faint, barely audible voice coming from the ladder.

"Edward?"

They all turned to locate the source and found Santini hanging desperately onto the stanchion, dead white, his eyes like black studs driven into his face.

Animal left his seat and hurried over to him. "What's the matter, buddy?" he said, taking Santini's arm.

"My system," Santini moaned, looking as if he had been crying. "Someone stole my system."

"Stole your system?"

"The notebook's not in the room. It's not anywhere. I must ask you, Edward: did you have anything to do with it?"

Animal was ready to protest when Santini interrupted him. "You've often said that it was a waste of time. I thought perhaps you were trying to do me a favor."

"I didn't take it, Santini."

"You understand why I had to ask—"

"Sure, sure." Animal led him back to the table. Who in hell would do such a thing? The system wasn't even *working,* for Christ's sake. He leaned over and muttered to the others, so the spectators couldn't hear.

"Somebody swiped Santini's system, his note pad. Anybody know who did it?"

"I'd have thought about it—if he was ahead," Augie said. "But now—"

"You would. Hubbard?"

"I just don't see the logic in it."

"Me either . . . Cowboy?"

"When did it happen?" Charlie asked.

Santini said it must have been when he was in the shower.

"Where were you, Podberoski, when he was taking a shower?" Augie wanted to know.

"Goosin' him with the soap, you idiot. I was right there with him."

"He was," Santini verified.

"Well, Hubbard and I were in our room," said Augie.

"Looks like I'm the outlaw then," Charlie said. "I didn't see anybody before breakfast."

"Don't sweat it," Animal said. "You're the last guy who'd need to do this. My canary is a better suspect."

"So what do we do?"

What *could* they do? Search the ship? Threaten two hundred and fifty men? With what? *If Santini's notes don't turn up by three o'clock, you'll all be . . .* Who had access to the room other than the players? Anybody could have strolled by, zipped in and out with the notebook. But why?

Augie motioned Larry Kettle over.

"Kettle, were you anywhere near Santini's room about an hour ago?"

"No."

"Where were you?"

"Setting up down here."

"Who is normally near the rooms around that time?"

Kettle thought a minute. "Nobody in particular."

"And everybody in general," Augie added.

"The question is whether Santini wants to continue playing," said Hubbard.

"Think about that, Santini," Animal said. "You were doin' shitty with the notes; without them you might shake up the cards."

"I don't know . . ."

"Or you can take what you got left and spend it in a better place."

Santini knew that without his system he had no reference point . . . yet he had watched the system break down, which meant, in logical terms, that the system *was* doing him no good, in fact was doing him harm. With the system his chances were poor. Perhaps without it, he would recoup his losses.

"I'm in," he said, straightening up in his chair.

For the next few hours Santini's small pile of cash grew smaller. He played as if he wanted to lose, chasing after hands he had no business chasing, staying when he should have dropped. He overbet. He tried filling inside straights.

It was as if he were waiting for some magical benefactor to suddenly perch on his shoulder.

Still, by eight in the evening, with the game slated to break up at ten, Santini was still in, and had, in fact, just gathered in two small pots in a row—maybe his benefactor had finally made an appearance.

As the dealer, Charlie Buck threw out the first round of cards face down, the second up. Animal was high with a king and bet $2,000. Santini and Charlie covered the bet. Hubbard and Augie folded.

On the next card Animal showed a nine to go with his king while Santini had a nine and ten of different suits. Charlie was low with a two-six.

Still high on the board, Animal shoved $3,000 into the pot; Santini and Charlie matched him. The fourth card fell.

Animal got another nine, giving him a pair. Santini caught a second ten. Charlie drew a second deuce. Santini had the top pair showing with his tens.

"Bet the monster," Animal told him, and Santini deposited a conservative two thousand dollars in the center.

Charlie slid in his two grand, and raised three more.

Animal wondered what the hell the Cowboy could have—another six in the hole? Another two? Animal remembered Hubbard and Epstein's cards before they folded. No help there.

"I'm in," Animal said, sliding in the $5,000.

Santini also called, leaving him with almost nothing.

Last card.

Animal caught a jack of clubs, Santini a five, and Charlie a queen.

Santini's pair of tens was still high. He looked at Animal's nines and Charlie's twos and knew if he'd had the system with him he could have figured out the only rational move. He had them beat on the board, but what were their hole cards like?

"Check," he said.

Charlie glanced at Santini's nearly depleted pile of cash and said, "One thousand dollars," knowing that the little fella didn't have much more than that.

Animal found himself in a predicament: would Santini bet his last thousand against the possibility of Charlie beating him?

"I know it's a whole thousand dollars, Mister Podberoski." Charlie smiled. "You want to consult with the troops back here?"

"At ease, Cowboy. I'm thinkin'." Then, after another few moments, he said, "All right, I'm in."

Now it was up to Santini. A thousand wasn't much compared to the half million dollars on the table, but it was a lot of money when that's all the money he had. Besides, he was more than halfway convinced that either Charlie or Podberoski held better hands than were showing on the board . . . On the other hand, going into the next hand with just a thousand dollars meant a game of showdown for sure against the four other players. Balancing the odds, he decided he was better off investing his thousand now.

"All right," he said. "I'll call you, Charlie."

"C'mon, Cowboy," Animal said, "let's see the powerhouse."

"You do see it," Charlie said, indicating his deuces.

"Fuck!" Animal shouted. "You were fuckin' bluffing!"

A quick smile snapped across Santini's face as he tapped his pair of tens—the winners—and raked in the pot.

Animal leaned across the table at Charlie. "Why'd you do that?"

"To irritate yuh." Charlie smiled.

"You did a good job."

Santini proceeded to win another two pots, small ones, but sufficient enough to build his confidence. At nine-thirty, just a half hour before quitting time, he caught his first big hand in a long time—$25,000—by edging Hubbard's nine-high straight with his own jack-high, which he celebrated by tipping Kettle's messboys with hundred-dollar bills.

On what turned out to be the final hand of the night, Animal dealt. The betting commenced, with Charlie and Hubbard folding right away and Animal dropping after the third card, leaving Santini and Augie in a head-to-head battle.

After four cards the hands looked like this:

SANTINI	AUGIE
hole card	hole card
9 clubs	J diamonds
5 hearts	8 diamonds
9 hearts	9 diamonds

Santini didn't have to leaf through his cash to know that he had exactly $53,000. A quick glance across the table told him that Augie was working on a flush, possibly a straight flush, but with the seven of diamonds having already fallen, the chances for that were nearly gone.

As a strict percentage shot Santini knew that this was the time for a crucial play: he had a five in the hole, and his nine and fives were indisputable winners to this point.

He could bet a nominal figure of, say, ten thousand, which Augie would certainly match on the chance that he'd catch his flush, or he could make the only sensible wager: bet all of it, and hopefully chase Augie away.

Santini riffled through his cash, then cupped his hands

behind the pile and eased the entire $53,000 into the center, announcing the figure.

There was an instant burst of chatter from the spectators, then the noise died down as they waited to see Augie's next move.

Augie sat very still with his back flush against the chair, eyes fixed on his own hand, arms folded over his chest. He knew precisely how much money there was in his stack—$66,000—which meant if he matched Santini's bet and lost he would be reduced to $13,000. But he could not be concerned with losing; rather, he concentrated on the fact that only one other diamond had fallen, the seven.

Animal, who usually tried to speed up the game, said nothing, for he knew exactly what Augie was going through.

Augie began to pick at the crown of his head; his forehead became creased, three deep canals stretching from one side to the other. His intuition told him to call the bet.

"Call," he said from behind his dark glasses, counting out $53,000 and dropping it in. Santini shot a quick, anxious glance at him.

"Last card," Animal said, "here we go. Santini"—he turned over the card, another five—"two pair."

Santini didn't mask his expression: it was all over his face—a full house. Augie didn't mask his either, as he sank further into his chair, picking more furiously at his scalp.

"And for Eppy," Animal said, "queen of diamonds. Flush time." Which made no difference, a full house beats a flush all day long.

"It's your bet, Santini," Animal said, "but since you ain't got nothin' left, you both might as well turn over your cards."

Santini dropped his head back and with a grand display turned over his hole card, the third five. He had it, the full house: 5-5-5-9-9.

He reached forward to pull in the pot when Augie said, "Hold it," and flipped over his own hole card, the ten of diamonds. A flush. A *straight* flush. 8-9-10-J-Q of diamonds. A winner.

The wail erupting from Santini could have broken glass, and the color that had returned to his face over the past few hours abruptly drained away. Stiff as a department-store mannequin, he kept his eyes fixed on the pile of cash that Augie dragged into his corner. Not a word was spoken, not even by Animal, who wanted desperately to console him but knew whatever he said would make no difference.

Santini remained this way while Hubbard motioned Kettle over. The players counted out their money before depositing it in the brown satchel and were about to get up from the table when Santini rose first, bowing to each man.

"Thank you, gentlemen," he said with great dignity, and marched out of the hold.

Chapter Six

THAT EVENING after another nearly inedible supper, Augie left his quarters at 11:15 and took a stroll forward, circling around the mainmast and jumbo boom, and down to the galley where he ran into the First Cook in the passageway.

"You, Cookie," Augie said, pointing a finger at him. "I want to talk to you."

"I am Fumi, no Cookie."

"I want to ask you a question."

Fumi took off the cap and squashed it into his rear pocket. His whites were filthy, nearly black with grease and grit and food stains and steak blood . . . steak blood?

Confirmed. Augie had completed half his mission—to locate the gourmet counter.

"On your sparkling uniform there is blood," he said. "You've noticed?"

Fumi inspected himself and saw the evidence.

"That's steak blood, Cookie, which means somewhere on this dreamboat is steak. Where?"

"No, no steak," Fumi protested.

"How about roast beef? Roast-beef blood?"

"No, no, no roast beef."

Augie snatched him up by the collar. Face to face, lips almost touching, Augie said to him: "You've served me rotten potatoes, your sandwiches I can't talk about without puking, the coffee . . .? What can I say, Cookie, sometimes it's brown, sometimes it isn't. It tastes like shit, which in fact it may be. I want to know the origin of that blood. I'll count to three. One—"

"I don't know. I don't know!"

Augie squeezed the collar around Fumi's neck.

"You know one reason I like steak? It makes me calm. It takes away the danger in me. Without it, I've been known to go mad. I once killed a guy for steak, my best friend."

Fumi didn't know whether to believe that or not, but the soldier certainly looked ready to belt somebody.

"Two—"

Fumi thought fast. Should he take the chance of a broken jaw over Larry Kettle's fury? To whom was he more indispensible? To Kettle, obviously.

"Thr—"

"No . . . I will show you," and Augie let him go.

Fumi led him into the galley, by the main freezer and into a storeroom, where a second freezer was housed, hidden behind a shelf of canned goods.

Inside the freezer, Augie found two sides of beef hanging from hooks. A network of steel runners ran overhead, designed to carry the hooks' rollers into position.

"What's the weight?"

"Three hundred pound."

"Three hundred pounds of beef. For what?"

"For you," Fumi said nervously, his yellow teeth peeking through.

"Then why haven't I been getting any?"

Fumi shrugged. "No can tell."

"Who does that meat belong to?"

"The purser, Mister Kettle," he said meekly.

"No kidding."

"I have told you nothing," Fumi said nervously. "You have not talked to Fumi, yes?"

"Never heard of you," Augie said, leaving the galley in search of Larry Kettle.

Larry Kettle owned the dubious distinction of possibly being the smallest purser in the entire Merchant Marine. His face was a swamp of freckles that matched the color of his hair perfectly, hair that rolled wave-like over his forehead and on occasion over his eyes. He was forty but looked ten years younger, and from the way he spoke —lazy Kentuckian hills—one might wonder how he had risen to his position as third in command of the *John Logan*, behind Chief Mate Sam Murphy and Captain James X. O'Roark. (O'Roark had been drunk in his stateroom from the time the ship left port.)

Kettle had been delighted to learn that a half-million-dollar poker game would be held on his ship. It was his last voyage, and wouldn't this be something to tell the folks back home! He had taken great pleasure in accommodating the players with whatever conveniences he could: supervising their meals, cleaning their uniforms, whatever . . . it kind of made him feel like an impressario.

His personal favorite among the players was Charlie Buck, with whom he shared a certain affinity for the country life. In fact, it was one of Charlie's cowboy outfits that he carried over his arm now as he left the laundry and started up toward the accommodations.

When he rounded the corner, however, he found himself looking up into Augie Epstein's smiling face.

"Mr. Kettle, how are you?" Augie said pleasantly.

"Jes' fine, yourself?" he replied, but when he started by he felt Augie's hand on his shoulder.

"Did you know," Augie said, turning and walking alongside him, "that just a few short months ago a Belgian could sell a German a can of coffee for three hundred Reichsmarks?"

"That a fact?"

"Yes it is."

They reached the ladder. Kettle climbed up first, Augie right behind him.

"Did you also know," Augie continued in the same cordial tone, "that within the last few weeks twenty-five thousand tons of black-market butter changed hands in Paris, and that bombed bridges held up legal goods while black-market trucks crossed rivers like magic?"

Kettle shot a sidelong glance at him and kept moving.

"Interestin'," he said.

"And that whole trainloads of food have been reported lost, including the locomotives?"

"Really, now."

"Have you heard about that big black-market gang of AWOL troops, about seventeen thousand of them, running loose and hijacking cigarettes, tires, jeeps, whatever they can get their hands on, run by OSS guys from their Parisian offices?"

"Can't say that I have."

Augie moved ahead of Kettle and blocked his way.

"Have you ever heard of Rabbit Toland, Mr. Kettle?"

Kettle repeated the name—not that he could recall. "Who is he?"

"Rabbit Toland was the purser on the Liberty Ship

Robert Louis Stevenson—sold eight hundred jeeps to the Krauts in Sicily."

"I seem to re—"

"Old Rabbit was caught and tried in Rome. But he was innocent as a lamb, he hold me, wanted the world press to know that. Then he told me about Merchant Marine pursers who weren't so innocent."

Kettle smiled up at him, then, with a befuddled look, said, "Why is it you're tellin' me this, Corporal?"

"By way of an introduction, Mr. Kettle, to inquire as to the reason why three hundred pounds of beef are hanging in your back freezer."

He caught a sudden flicker of uncertainty in Kettle's eyes. "What beef?" he said.

"Two sides of beef, on hooks."

"What gives you that idea, Corporal?"

"Never reveal your source, that's an old newspaper adage."

"I got an old adage for you, Epstein," Kettle said. "Mind your own business and you won't have no problems."

"What about the beef, Mister Kettle?"

"What about it? I own it. I paid for it. It's mine."

Augie was leaning with his back against the ladder, preventing Kettle from climbing up.

"Then let me put it to you this way," he said. "You have men dying in sick bay. You have two hundred and some-odd troops on this tub being fed slop because you probably sold all the good food to a black-marketeer. If just one of those troops learns about that beef, you'll have a mutiny on your hands. You want that?"

Kettle offered no reply, standing his ground and waiting for Augie to continue.

"What I'm suggesting is this," Augie told him. "You

sell the beef to us players, have it served up in the rooms, if you like. That way nobody will know."

"Well now, that's damn decent of you, Epstein—what with all your talk about the poor men dying in sick bay, you want me to give it to the players."

Augie had the urge to ask him why Fumi had steak blood on his whites but decided to honor his promise to the cook.

"That's exactly what I want you to do, Kettle."

"All three hundred pounds?"

"No, just one of the sides will do. There are five of us. With one meal a day, with a pound or two per steak, not counting the fat, one of the sides should suffice. You can keep the other one."

Kettle considered that for a moment, realizing he didn't have much say in the matter.

"You know that other old adage, Epstein, about one rotten apple spoiling the rest."

"I do, and I'm trying to keep you from being that rotten apple, Kettle. You should thank me for looking out for your well-being. Are you going to sell me the beef?"

Kettle's freckles seemed to compress over the bridge of his nose. "I'll sell it to you."

"And by the way," Augie said, indicating Charlie's clothes, which Kettle had squashed in his anger. "You'd better give those another press."

Wordlessly, Kettle did an about-face and stalked back in the direction of the laundry.

"Oh, and Kettle . . ." Augie's voice called from behind.

"Yeah, what?"

"The steak," Augie said with a grin. "I like mine medium rare."

Chapter Seven

EVAN HUBBARD spent between midnight and one that
night in the john composing a letter—it was the only
place he could get any privacy—and then went to bed.
An hour later he was awakened by the dream again. He'd
had it every night he'd been on the ship.

In the nightmare he grappled with the RAF Major
again outside a Casablanca café, and the Major reeled
back and fell dead in the street—only it wasn't the Major
at all, but Hubbard's father, Major General Evan Hubbard III. At the very last instant his father's face sup-
planted that of the major's, and Hubbard clutched the
gun, homing in for the kill—

The nightmare was terrifying enough for him to cry
out and startle Augie out of a deep sleep and to keep
Hubbard awake, soaked with perspiration, until the Casablanca street that lingered in his vision gradually meta-
morphosed into the dull grayness of his quarters. Slowly,
the jackhammer pace of his heartbeat and his breathing

receded, and his eyelids, which felt leaden, slowly opened to extinguish the patricide. He propped the pillow behind his head and, lying on his back, wondered how many *more* times he would improvise the death of his father.

A doctor friend in Casablanca, with whom he'd spent many hours, had explained that one of the most difficult things in the world was to be brought up perfect, by seemingly perfect parents, whose own perfect ancestry dated back to Jamestown. In such cases, he said, it was fashionable family tradition to loathe one's own father.

Hubbard had explained to the friend that the General had done everything humanly possible to ingratiate his son—money, education, plush military assignments.

"Which is the very reason you hate him," the friend had told him. "He's never let you do anything on your own."

To which Hubbard had had to agree. The General had even assigned a spy, one Colonel James Morley, to the Consulate in order to report back on his activities. But Hubbard had been on to Morley right away. Lord, the things he'd done to infuriate the General.

In particular, gambling.

Gambling provided the means by which Hubbard freed himself financially. Even at the age of twelve he had been sneaking behind the country-club stables to play cards with older kids, gambling with the meager allowance bestowed by his father and the money his mother gave him on the sly. And he had won rather large amounts sometimes, which even then he had stashed away with an eye toward future independence.

So this game should have been it, the final roadblock to overcome so he could be totally independent. But something was going wrong. The psychological shift between escaping the burden of his father and making it on his own was simple—but it was not so simple to erase the truth that he was in abject fear of the man, a fear that had accelerated during the last few days.

The RAF Major's death had resurrected the fear ... Charlie Buck's monumental card playing was converting it into a monster.

"If I don't win," Hubbard had caught himself muttering, "I'll turn into another Santini." Fear of losing now obsessed him, and wasn't it bitterly ironic, he thought, that the very thing that promised to sever the umbilical cord—gambling—now threatened to bind him further, for he knew that arriving in New York penniless would drive him home to Virginia and his father's "I told you so." Which for a twenty-eight-year-old man who was brought up to be perfect was the real sacrilege, a failure in the most profound sense of the word.

Whatever the cost, he knew he could not allow that to happen ... and the only way to prevent a journey back was to call on every weapon in his poker-playing arsenal to squash Charlie Buck.

Animal Podberoski had learned to sleepwalk as a kid, and his parents had often found him in the morning fast asleep on the toilet seat, so it was no wonder that he was barely aware now, just before sunrise, of having crawled out of the sack and stumbled down the corridor to the head.

His trenchcoat parted around him, barefoot and freezing, he had eased his ass carefully onto the cold seat, and after the initial shock, the motion of the ship had gently rocked him from side to side, lulling him back to sleep. To avoid the light shining directly into his face he slumped forward, elbows supported on his knees.

Then something caught his eye, on the floor, under

the metal divider between the stalls. It looked like a couple of folded sheets of paper, and after staring at them for a while, he reached down and picked them up with a round, sluggish curl of his arm.

It was a letter, addressed to:

Major General Evan Hubbard III
American Embassy
London

Father,

Read this letter carefully because it has been a long time in the making. First off, let me say that I am writing you from aboard a ship, on which a half-million-dollar poker game is in progress. I am one of the players.

Furthermore, I am (and have been for a long time) aware that you transferred Colonel Morley to the Casablanca Consulate with instructions to spy on me and my activities, at which he failed, but with good faith. Thank God you are not in espionage.

Thirdly, I heard quite by accident (but from excellent sources) that you are openly running around with and bedding nearly a platoon (the sources' word) of English secretaries while your wife and my mother sits back at Mirabelle. Who you sleep with is your own business but, for Christ's sake (or Mother's), heed your own words: Discretion is the better part of valor, or Honor Above All, or any of those other platitudes you used to drum into me. They weren't platitudes, as it turned out—*you* are, you hypocrite. Getting madder, are you?

Next: You no longer have to keep an eye on me. Send no more spies. Do me no more favors. In other words, lay off. I'm a big boy now. Nearly twenty-nine. Remember? Now let's talk about the notion of one of your favorite topics: masculinity . . .

Masculinity? What about it? Animal looked for another page but that was all there was. Clutching his
trenchcoat he clomped around in his boots searching
for more: under the stalls, behind the johns, under the
sinks. Nothing.

"Fucking Hubbard!" he said out loud. Just when he
was getting interested.

Back on the john, he considered what exactly to do
with this spicy material: leave it here for somebody else
to pick up and spread rumors about Hubbard and his old
man? Throw it away? Hand it to Hubbard personally?

Ah, no. He knew precisely what to do with the pages,
and a few minutes later was standing outside Hubbard's
room, checking to see if he and Epstein were asleep.

They were. Animal quietly stepped out of his boots
and, with his teeth clenched and eyes scanning the darkness, tiptoed inside to Hubbard's wall locker and placed
the pages on the top shelf.

In his own bunk a few minutes later he lay awake,
thinking about Hubbard . . . and devising methods to use
the letter against him . . .

The first thing Animal saw when he opened his eyes
the next morning at eight-thirty was Santini, seated on
the edge of his bunk, looking as if he was in the midst
of cardiac arrest. Animal pretended to be still asleep, but
through the slits in his eyes he saw that Santini's hair,
which used to be slicked back and neat as a pin, was
springing out of his scalp like electrician's wires. Both
hands hovered over his knees, the fingers floating around
as if he were molding clay. Animal couldn't even see
his eyes, they had retreated so far back in their sockets—
he could tell, however, that the eyes were interested in
whatever his fingers were making out of the air.

"Santini?"

No reaction.

Animal cleared his throat and tried again.

"Santini!"

The head snapped up as if the voice had come from above.

"What!"

"Over here."

"Yes, Edward." His voice was hollow, nearly an echo, it seemed so far away.

Animal threw the covers off and, swinging his legs over the side, sat facing Santini.

"It can't be all that bad, buddy. I mean, Christ, you're goin' home. You can get your old job back teachin' math, right? You got your folks. Then you got the States, which you ain't been back to in . . . how long?"

"Oh, I don't know. Seven years or so, maybe less."

"You're due."

Animal stood and stretched and on his way to his locker pulled the cover off the bird cage, lighting up the day for Poncho, who celebrated by leaping from bar to bar, singing at the top of his lungs.

"Good morning, sweetheart." Animal ran his fingers over the cage, waving at the bird. "I got some breakfast for you."

After feeding Poncho, Animal reached inside the locker and pulled out a bulky envelope, which he carried back to his bunk.

"Listen, Santini," he said in his most empathetic voice, "I know how much you wanted to take some money home to your folks."

"My folks are dead."

"Gee, I'm sorry to hear . . . Then I know how much you wanted to maybe invest in a small business—"

"Poker's my business, Edward."

"Whaddya mean, poker's your business? You told me you were a math professor."

"Years ago."

"What about in the service, what about—"

Santini interrupted him with a wave of the hand. "I worked for the OSS, Edward, my cover was as a poker player. How do you think I participated in those big private games. I was recruited into the OSS for my ability with figures, and poker became a natural offshoot. As it turned out, poker became my profession, and the OSS a sort of hobby."

"Then why didn't you stay over there, Santini? It sounds like you had it made."

"The same reason you didn't stay, Edward—this game. I wanted to match my ability against yours, for the half million dollars."

"Well, yeah, but . . . wait a minute, I'm losing my train of thought." He pulled a cigar out and struck a match against the stanchion. "If your folks are dead and you don't want a business or to teach math, and here you are out of the game, whaddya going to do with your life?"

"Difficult to explain, Edward."

"Go ahead, I got time."

"In Eastern philosophy," Santini began, "I—"

"Not *that* much time." Animal knew he had to be careful not to let Santini drift off; he also knew that the only way to keep Santini's mind on the real world was to keep the conversation active with quick one-line sentences. Santini was understandable at that level.

Santini continued:

"Simply put, then, as far as the immediate situation is concerned, understand that losing the money does not depress me, that I can no longer participate in the game *does*."

"Which means what, you're well heeled?"

"Oh, no, quite the contrary. I'm rather broke at the moment."

"In that case, Santini, I got something I wanna talk to you about."

"What's that?"

Animal pulled the envelope out. "I didn't get a chance to tell you last night, but the other guys and me got together and . . ." He handed the envelope to him.

"What is it?"

"Open it and find out."

Santini held the envelope up to the light and surveyed its perimeters. He checked for a name and address. Clean. He tore it open.

"Be careful," Animal told him.

Out slid the contents: a wad of paper money. Santini fingered the bills as if looking for forgery, then riffled through the bills.

"Go ahead," Animal smiled, "count it."

Santini began stacking the bills one by one. They were in hundred-dollar denominations, but when it looked as if he would take forever, Animal said, "Forget it. There's eight thousand bucks."

From the way Santini fanned and stacked the bills it was obvious to Animal that he still hadn't gotten the message.

"What do you want me to do with these, Edward? They're not phony as far as I can tell. I could inspect them more closely if you'd like."

"Santini, they're real. They're not for you to inspect, they're for you to have. The guys and I took up a little collection and here yuh go."

Santini returned the bills to the envelope and handed it back. "I can't accept this. This is not the way one plays poker. One doesn't . . . pay back losers. That's not Hoyle."

Animal stared at the envelope suspended between them but wouldn't reach for it. "Tell yuh what," he said, leaning forward, puffing on his cigar. "You show me where Hoyle says you can't take a donation and I'll take it back."

"Edward, this is so generous of you all, but—"

A whistle sounded from topside, a service of Larry Kettle, indicating that the game would start in half an hour.

Talking rapidly now, Animal said, "It was the Cowboy's idea to give you the money. The rest of us chipped in. I can't return it because they'll think I blew it, which would put me in a weak position with them, see? I can't let that happen, Santini, because I'm still in the game. And you know what else? Epstein will say, hey, I can make him take the dough and he'll be over here badgering you. Then you turn him down and Hubbard'll be here. Then the Cowboy himself. I can't sleep with people traipsing in and out of here like that. I need sleep, *you* need sleep—so you have to take it. Please?"

Santini heard the faint cry of logic. In matters of this sort he remembered his father telling him long ago that a first refusal means politeness, a second stupidity, a third showed serious mental decline.

"In that case, Edward," he said, "Thank you very much. I'll thank the others as well."

"Don't bother, I'll thank them for you. In fact, they don't want to be thanked. Now, enough."

As Animal went through the motions of getting ready to go down and play—brushing his teeth with the corner of his handkerchief, saying good-bye to Poncho—Santini tucked himself under the faded blue Navy blanket and came to the conclusion that the only logical reason for this gift was the players' belief that he had been victimized by the theft of his system, and he was grateful for their kindness.

"Santini?" he heard Animal say, and peeked over the covers.

"Yes, Edward?"

"I ain't one for the pot callin' the kettle black but you been real sloppy the last couple days. Think you could straighten up while I'm gone? 'Atta boy."

With that he left the room.

Chapter Eight

IT WAS SAID back in his native Montana that Charlie Buck could charm the teeth out of a coyote. It was also said, and this with a whisper, that Charlie himself was charmed, that his life was in some magical way protected by an ancient Indian shaman who used to ride across these very plains.

The people of Miles City had good reason to believe these things about Charlie because by the time he was fifteen he had been a sole survivor too many times *not* to believe.

He had been the only one to live through a cattle stampede, at eight. Two years later, skiing up in the Bitterfoot Range, a white-out blew off the peaks and of the thirty-eight missing bodies the search parties found only his. At fourteen he shot the Milk River rapids with four buddies on a sturdy homemade raft and after it went down he spent a week in the woods before he could find somebody to tell his story to.

And these were just a few of the reasons why the people of Miles City nicknamed him Lucky Charlie Buck.

"It's all very logical, my boy," said his Uncle Dandy. "Your good fortune brings others misfortune. People suffer from your luck, Charlie, they're victimized by it. When you win, they lose. But you must understand something: you are not suddenly blessed by good fortune— in reality you remain steady. It's their *bad* luck. You generate bad luck, Charlie, you lucky boy."

But for all his charm and boyish good looks and his disarming smile, the men with whom he sat down at the poker table had been able to tell right off that Charlie Buck was no easy mark. Veterans like Podberoski and Santini had seen a million kids come and go, like pinwheels, burning out in a hurry and going away, but not this one. At twenty-three—they talked about it and agreed—Charlie was better than they were at thirty.

The consensus was that Charlie knew how to handle the streak he was riding, and for a guy that young to handle it that well was like a piece of art, or, as Santini put it, a magnificent Bordeaux with years of maturity ahead of it.

"It's like playing against God," was Augie's comment.

However, by four that afternoon, the inevitability of Charlie Buck winning it all was no longer apparent. Up on deck the soldiers not attending the game heard rumors of a major shift in power.

In the past hour Charlie had lost three hands, two to Hubbard and one to Augie Epstein, to the tune of $80,000. The absence of Santini, so popular opinion went, had upset the rhythm of the game. Acknowledging the shift, Charlie was calling for a fresh deck on nearly every hand in an attempt to restore his winning ways, but the tactic had backfired on him in the most devastating way possible. The cards he drew were too good to fold but not good enough to win, so he kept finding himself in head-to-head battles with Hubbard and Epstein, each time coming up second best. The card play, which for four days had been tight as a rod, consequently loosened up—and Charlie was the one being stalked now.

After dropping close to $35,000 on the previous hand, Charlie, knowing a quick resurrection was out and desperate to find some other way to break the fall, excused himself and went off to the john.

Augie waited for him to leave before hoisting his coffee cup in a toast.

"Gentlemen," he said, removing his sunglasses, "to the transposition of fate. It's about time."

"I'd like to drink to that," Animal said, "but I ain't seen none of that fate transposed over here."

"Don't worry about it," Augie assured him, "you'll get yours."

Animal struck a match to his cigar and, looking at Hubbard, casually changed the subject, "You know, Hubbard, you look a lot like wha'shisname, the king who gave up his throne to marry that American broad."

"The Duke of Windsor."

"Yeah, that's the guy. You ever been to England?"

"On occasion."

"Yeah? What do you think of them British secretaries?"

Animal watched very closely for some indication that Hubbard had linked up the question with the letter to his father, but found nothing.

"Why do you ask?" said Hubbard.

"What, I gotta explain all my questions? All right, Eppy, what do *you* think about British secretaries?"

Augie shrugged, "In bed?"

"Listen to the filthy mind over here. All right, in bed."

"They're not clean. They have blotchy skin and all

their teeth are rotten, and they're great fucks. Now I have a question for you. What exactly happened to you and Santini in that Antwerp whorehouse?"

"Nothin' you would have lived through. We were ambushed by these Nazi-type goons and their broads. They chased us over broken glass and down mountains, and all we had on were bathrobes. In five years of battle I never came so close to death."

"What about you beating up the whore and not paying her?"

"Pure rumor."

Augie persisted. "You mean to tell me those whores and their pimps chased you all that way for no good reason?"

"I didn't like the broad, Epstein. I thought I was gettin' something better and I got pissed. I didn't beat her up, I tied her up, and, that's right, I didn't give her one fuckin' nickel, but that's her tough luck because what I contracted for I didn't get. End of story."

"C'mon, Pod," Augie whispered confidentially, "you can tell the truth to the son of a rabbi. Admit it. You couldn't get it up."

"Do I hear an echo in here! End of Story means End of Story!"

Charlie meanwhile ambled back to the table and, taking up the deck, offered Animal the cut.

"Okay," Charlie said with the same easy smile, "I lightened my load and got my confidence back, fellas, so from now on I'm gon' be tough to beat."

"Thank you, Mr. Rockne. Deal the cards."

They decided to up the ante to $1,000, which of course meant they had a larger stake in each pot now, compelling them to think twice about folding right away.

Charlie dealt, calling out the cards as they fell.

Animal was high and bet $5,000. Charlie and Hubbard called. Augie folded, adding, "Didn't I tell you, Podberoski? You'll get yours."

"Which makes you a prophet either way. Next card, Cowboy."

After the third card fell and Charlie dropped, it was left to Animal and Hubbard.

"You were stationed down in Casablanca, Hubbard, that right?" Animal said.

"That's right. I'll bet five thousand."

"Did you ever run across an old friend of mine down there by any chance—a Colonel Morley?"

Hubbard perked up with that question. "You know Colonel Morley?"

"Yeah, sure, the sonofabitch . . . biggest rat I ever knew. Used to work for generals, spy kind of shit, keeping his eye on certain guys and reporting back."

"How do you know Morley?" Hubbard said, forgetting the hand for the moment.

"You fellas still playin cards or what?" Charlie asked.

"I knew him through these British secretaries," Animal said. "I knew a whole fuckin' platoon of them up there in London, used to hang around the American Embassy sleeping with the generals."

"It's your bet, Podberoski," Charlie insisted. "Five thousand. You in?"

"In? Not like them generals were in those British secretaries." Animal laughed.

What's going on here, Hubbard thought.

"As a matter of fact," Animal said, seeming to remember something. "Hubbard . . . I know that name. Did I hear that your old man was a general somewhere, Captain?"

"Yes, that's right."

"Where's he stationed?"

Hubbard's face was blank, his eyes staring hard at Animal.

"London," he said.

"*That's* where I heard about them British secretaries. Your old man . . . say, how's your mother feel about—"

Wordlessly, Hubbard leapt from his seat and threw a right cross that caught Animal flush on the chin. If Animal's chair hadn't been bolted down, the blow would have sent him reeling back against the bulkhead. Instead, Hubbard hit him again, this time under his eye. Hubbard's body was flat across the table, his height enabling him to get at Animal again and again. Animal's head kept rocking back and then, like a spring, shooting back into place.

By the time Charlie and Augie were able to get into the fight Hubbard's face was directly over Animal's, his hands wrapped around his neck. Animal gagged and coughed as a trickle of blood oozed from the corner of his mouth.

Charlie managed to grab Hubbard's hands and, with Augie's help, pulled them off Animal's neck. With Charlie on one of Hubbard's arms and Augie on the other they yanked him back to his seat.

"Now stay there!" Augie screamed, blocking his view of Animal.

Hubbard's knuckles were white, his cheeks puffed and his eyes still murderous with rage. It took all his willpower not to launch himself across the table at the bastard again.

Animal, on the other hand, obviously looked as if he'd been on the wrong end of a massacre. His left eye had swollen enough to block his vision, and his jaw, from which Charlie had wiped the blood, felt as if it'd been given a massive dose of novocaine.

Meanwhile, Kettle scrambled around, gathering up the scattered bills, asking the players how much they had had, wiping up the spilled coffee. Within a few minutes the table had settled down, though Animal had trouble concentrating on anything but sitting up straight.

"I'm gonna say this quick," he said to Hubbard. "You listenin'?"

"Yes."

"First, a professional card player don't belt another professional card player, no matter what passes back and forth across the table. Which means you fucked up. This here's a mental game, Hubbard, not a prizefight." He licked his lips, still tasting the blood.

"Second. If you don't know it by now then you ain't been payin' attention. I play Intimidation Poker, Hubbard, which means I take my shots wherever I can, just as you do, and Augie and the Cowboy here. If you dish it out you also take it."

"Professional card players don't make slurs against—"

"Horseshit! What kinda games you been in, for crissakes? There ain't nothin' off limits. If I wanna call you an asshole, you either live with it or get the fuck out. Just because you're the silent type don't mean I have to be. A lotta different minds workin' here, a lotta different ways. This is for a half a million bucks, Hubbard, which means anything goes, short of pulling a gun—which I think you woulda done if you had one. You better straighten up, my friend, because from now on I'm gonna unload shit on you you never dreamed of. Now, where were we?"

They finished the hand with Animal winning on a pair of kings.

Whatever else the fight had done to the game, it did nothing to impede Charlie's downward trek. By the end of the evening he had dropped just under $100,000, leaving him with $145,000. Hubbard remained about the same and deposited $130,000 into his satchel for the night. Animal and Augie had pushed steadily forward until they had climbed over the $100,000 mark.

The rumor of a power shift was now an actuality. What had seemed like Charlie's own private domain yesterday had leveled off. When the players showed up tomorrow morning they would be playing almost even— as if it were the first day . . .

The gratitude in Santini screamed to be let out. Later that evening, he spotted Charlie Buck ambling along the corridor, and, easing up to him, said confidentially, "Charlie can I speak with you a moment?"

"Yeah, Santini, how yuh doin'?"

"Fine." He glanced up and down the passageway, then dragged Charlie into the john. "I know you don't want to be thanked for the eight thousand dollars, but I must thank you. It was very considerate of you and I appreciate it."

"Whaddya talkin' about?"

"Oh, go ahead and pretend. I'm just so overwhelmed by your generosity, by everybody's generosity, that I had to say something. I hope you understand."

Charlie's eyes shifted nervously, wondering if Santini had finally gone off the deep end.

"I understand why you and the others chose Edward to deliver the contribution. He was the obvious one, bunking in with me and all."

"The contribution?"

"But don't you worry, I promise not to say a word to Epstein or Hubbard. And please, whatever you do, don't tell Edward that I mentioned anything about it. Promise?"

Charlie shrugged. "Sure."

Santini reached for Charlie's hand and shook it hard, then stepped back from Charlie, smiled quickly and scurried around him, away from him, down the corridor.

Charlie wondered what the hell that was all about. Eight thousand dollars? Contribution? Podberoski? Catching himself in the mirror, he straightened his string tie. Poor Santini. The little fella had taken his last train ride out. Maybe he'd better go have a talk with Podberoski, ask him if it wouldn't be a good idea to have the doc take a look at Santini, maybe give him some medicine to calm him down.

A fella running around like that could be dangerous.

Chapter Nine

AT TWO IN THE MORNING of the seventh day the *John Logan* was struggling through high seas at ten knots. Rain pelted her decks as the bow plunged and rose, her hull creaking and straining against the increasing turbulence.

Chief Mate Sam Murphy had chosen sick bay to catch a wink before making his rounds, but at two-fifteen he bolted straight up in his berth. The ship was under attack! Plasma bottles and lamps swung like pendulums, bandages and splints and bottles of anesthetics everywhere. He saw medical aides strapping their patients in, operating tables being prepared for battle casualties.

Still groggy with sleep but with the single-minded purpose of making it to his station on the bridge, Murphy buttoned his pea jacket and started up the ladder—at which point he realized this was no battle raging up above, but one king hell of a storm.

A towering, serpent-like wave greeted him at the top of the ladder and he just had time to clutch harder at the ladder poles before the wave crashed over him. Gasping, he let go of the ladder and inched forward along the rail, then dropped into a crouch and tucked his head between his knees as he spotted another wave roaring in.

The wave slammed into him like a brick wall and he felt as if his back had snapped in two. This time his recovery took longer but with the bridge in sight and his Hail Marys to protect him, he took his bearings from the flashes of lightning crisscrossing above him. Soldiers tumbled by him, carried by the shifting river of surf, invisible except for the small red lights blinking on their life jackets.

For every step he took he was driven back three, but slowly, dodging waves, he wormed his way along the deck and over the engine casing, angling for the ladder that would take him to the bridge.

From the way the ship listed, Murphy knew that this was no ordinary Atlantic storm but a full-fledged terror, one such as he hadn't seen in years. He hoped to God the radio was still intact and its operator signaling his SOS, whatever good that would do—any ships in the area were undoubtedly having their own problems.

Reaching the foot of the ladder, and waiting there until it was safe to scramble up, he cursed Charlie Buck for shooting that damn seagull.

Down in the galley Fumi and his messboys had been jabbering away in Tagalog when the storm hit. The suddenness of the storm had scattered them and now, instead of securing the stores, they were fighting to keep the galley from flooding.

Cradling his cat under his arm, Fumi waded through pots and pans toward the lower food lockers and discovered the bad news. Not only had the crates been torn open and the food ruined, but the rusted door hinges had given way, allowing tons of water to surge in. The main meat locker had reached a similar fate: its hinges, too, had broken off and the meat inside looked as if it had been gnawed apart by giant sets of teeth.

As Fumi inspected the remains of his small private kingdom he emitted a steady, high-pitched whine, shaking his cat as if it were responsible for the disaster, blinking away the tears or the drops of salt water that were stinging his eyes. He kept at it, rummaging through the galley, trying to save whatever he could, but finally, giving up on the main room, he let the water sweep him along toward the small meat locker in the rear, where Kettle's beef hung. The locker, blockaded by crates of water-soaked vegetables and canned goods bobbing on the surface, seemed intact.

Convinced now there was nothing left for him to do but save his own life, he squeezed his cat further into his armpit and scaled the metal racks to the highest shelf, where he sat, his pinched yellow face bleak with misery, watching the water rise toward him.

Charlie Buck was already on deck.

Whatever had possessed him to come up here had started in sleep. Before he knew it he had climbed out of the sack, thrown on his clothes and pushed up into the storm, and now here he was in the middle of it, hanging onto the rail, positioned behind the uptake valves so he wouldn't be crushed by the mountains of surf rolling off the starboard bow.

It was the wildest damn thing he had ever seen, this storm, the way it swirled around him, like being on the inside of a tornado, and the sound it made, like timber falling but louder. And the water, like buzz saws slashing across his face and hands, right through his clothes, even.

And when he looked over the side, the sea came up to his feet sometimes as the ship leaned over and then rocked back so that he had to hang on tighter to keep from falling down.

He couldn't see anything except the sheets of water dashing by and the colors changing from gray to black to green, and every once in a while a bolt of lightning overhead. He didn't dare move for fear he'd be snapped up by the sea and disappear—but God, did he love this, he suddenly discovered, like riding some wild stallion that never ran out of steam. Jee-zuz! And to think he'd been scared of the sea.

"All I wanna know," said Sam Murphy when he burst into the wheelhouse, "is who didn't pay that Antwerp whore."

Larry Kettle was there, the radio operator beside him busy rapping out an SOS. He told Murphy that the bridge steering gear had gone out and the crewmen were fighting like hell to stay on course with emergency equipment from the after-platform. Murphy took the radio and ordered the engineer to slow down and the starboard anchor dropped—most likely a useless maneuver, but there was a chance the anchor might be able to stabilize the ship. The word came back that the anchor chain was stuck and Murphy sent three crewmen with hacksaws to cut it free.

Just then news came that a fire had started in the engine room that was certain to go out of control any minute, and worse, the hose lines had been burned through, and—communications between the wheelhouse and engine room abruptly stopped.

"Jesus H. Christ!" Murphy screamed. "Kettle, get your ass down there and find out what's going on."

"Murphy, I—"

"Move it!"

Kettle bundled up and pushed into the storm. The wind was up to seventy knots, and from what Murphy could see, the list was nearly thirty degrees. A crewman plowed in and reported that at least a dozen men had been swept overboard.

"Get them Army assholes to the boats. Knock 'em over the head if you have to."

The ship took a sudden drunken roll, hurling Murphy and his men to the deck.

"Flynn," he yelled to the operator, "anything on the SOS?"

"Nothing, sir."

Murphy knew he could no longer deceive himself— the ship was listing close to thirty-five degrees, it could capsize at any time . . . and the storm was still getting worse . . . He could no longer see out the wheelhouse window.

"Jesus, *somebody* answer our call," he mumbled. "The Navy, the Luftwaffe, *anybody* . . ."

Down in the engine room the First Mate and two men had calked the half-door but it wasn't holding; the door had been too eroded by rust. The shaft alley had to be oiled immediately, so the oiler was sent up on deck and down a narrow casing to the forward end of the alley. Sliding, gripping, moving crab-like, he finally reached the after escape hatch, but he was too big to climb up the ladder—the hatch was filled with team lines. Suddenly, one of the lines broke and burned away the oiler's face and hands, and, screaming, he fell backward and, caught by the flow of water, was carried off.

The starboard pumps had been drained, but under the reduced pressure the ship could heave up into the wind no more than a few degrees. The gang in the engine room worked at breakneck speed to keep the boilers going, but the steam kept dropping and finally hit zero. The machinery ground to a halt. The pumps failed, then the generators quit and all lights went off. The *John Logan* was now helpless and drifting.

Up top the decks were being pounded by seventy-five to one-hundred-foot waves, crashing in with a sound like metal being torn apart, burying the ship under thousands of tons of water. Sheets of sub-zero foam washed over the platforms. Part of the hull had cracked open along the welded seams, and the crack was widening. Murphy could hear his ship straining and groaning, and figured unless the storm let up soon they'd be going under.

The operator continued pounding out the SOS.

ENCOUNTERING SEVERE HURRICANE STOP SITUATION GRAVE STOP THIRTY-FIVE DE-GREE LIST AND SUFFERING STOP NEED HELP

With the generator knocked out, the message was being sent out on a battery-powered emergency set with a short-range capacity. Murphy prayed somebody would pick it up because another problem was developing. The ship was listing close to forty degrees now—and two hundred and fifty-seven troops were running out of air down in the holds.

Not only that, he had sent part of the deck crew to man the lifeboats but, count on the fucking Army, no-body seemed to have paid any attention to the boat drills. His men were on deck, shouting, "Lower away! Get the lifeboats out of here!" and nobody was responding.

Then the word came back to Murphy that none of the lifeboats on the port side could be lowered because of the bulge in the hull. Life-saving equipment was out of whack; the davits were rusted, the mechanism useless, hardened and clogged by an accumulation of grease and paint. Crank handles were missing, falls were tangled, many of them frayed and cut so short there wasn't enough rope to lower the boats all the way to the water. And finally, the list was so great the boats couldn't even be swung clear of the hull.

"Fuck it then!" he screamed. "Keep the troops below. Keep them balanced on either side of the holds. And forget Number Three, it's flooded."

As the crewman raced out Murphy saw a wave snap him across the deck and out of sight.

Charlie Buck had maneuvered himself to the afterdeck now, and was leaning over the rail, peering into the black hole of the sea. He had a firm grip on the railing, both legs braced against it for support. God! he kept repeating over and over. God! This is unbelievable!

He started to shift his position—when something exploded at the back of his neck, a blow too precise to have come from a wave. His knees buckled and he fell, still managing to hang on to the rail until he felt a second thud, this one near his right temple. Whatever strength he had left drained out of him. His vision clouded and turned black; he felt light-headed, as if the top of his skull had spun off into the storm. He was vaguely aware of two prong-like objects digging into his shoulders and pushing him down, and then he felt the railing slide out of his hands.

Quickly, the prongs crawled down his back and began easing him forward. He watched the railing pass overhead and then felt himself pushed over the edge and begin to fall.

His snap back to reality lasted just one second, at the instant he plunged into the water. He happened to be facing up toward the deck and saw standing there, his hands latched onto the rail, the figure of a man peering down at him.

Before the man on deck had a chance to turn and move away, Charlie Buck had been swallowed up by the sea.

By three the following day, the storm had passed. Teams of men had been working steadily for several hours, bailing out the holds and the engine room. The engineer and his crew had fixed the generator with parts delivered by a tanker that had pulled alongside around eleven. The *John Logan* had righted itself but the damage was so extensive Murphy knew he'd have to guide it into the New York harbor at no more than four knots.

Twenty-four men, including Charlie Buck, were reported missing. The medical crew had been beefed up to handle the sick and wounded.

Captain James X. O'Roark had slept through the storm. When he'd awakened at noon, he had been angry to find his cabin in disarray.

Animal Podberoski and Michelangelo Santini gathered up Charlie Buck's belongings, entrusting them to Larry Kettle.

The *John Logan,* according to Murphy's calculations, was three days out of New York. A formation gathered on the deck and prayers were said for the repose of the souls of the men who had perished at sea.

Chapter Ten

WITH THE POKER GAME POSTPONED because of flooding,
the players read or slept or gabbed with the troops.
Animal Podberoski had no time for such frivolities, however, because Santini had chosen—or had chosen for
him—this evening to seal his madness.

Santini's ramblings began alone as usual, then picked
up the pace once he had Animal as an audience. During
the last couple of days Animal had avoided the room
until late so that he might be spared his roomie's sudden
dashes into insanity.

This time, though, Animal had been drinking Scotch
with some soldiers he had met who had fought beside his
engineer battalion, and they'd spent hours trading stories
and lies and getting smashed. So by the time he walked
in at midnight he was feeling no pain and, in fact, was
actually looking forward to having a conversation with
Santini, whether he understood what he was saying or
not.

He found Santini cross-legged on his bed, like a

Buddha, his eyes rolled back in some kind of cosmic trance.

"What's up, Santini?" he said and, with a bottle of Scotch in one hand and his hat in the other, sat down on his bunk.

The Apocalypse, Santini explained, was up, so was something called simultaneous contrast, so was Rococo, Pousinistes and Rubenistes, to which Animal successively replied, "Oh, yeah?" and "No shit?" and "I can see what you mean," which of course he couldn't, but what did Santini care? The man was in communion with some higher plane.

"Edward," he finally said, with the first hint that he was actually talking to Animal, "I feel that I am entering a new consciousness, a state of neoteric logic, if you will, which by its obliteration of my past is purifying me. I can feel it, Edward."

"New?"

"Yes, new. I am becoming new."

"It's about fuckin' time. Except for the whorehouse, you been off on some tangent, Santini. Glad to see you gettin' back to normal—"

"Normal," Santini said, "in the metaphysical sense. In the past few months, I have witnessed the gradual disintegration of my memory, opening the way for my most profound cerebral expenditure."

Animal knew the only words he would get in were the ones he'd been interrupting with, so he said, "We all lose our memories sometimes. You can't expect to remember everything, I mean, I can hardly remember home, I been in the war so long."

"I remember my parents," said Santini, "probably because, having passed away, I am myself growing nearer to them."

"Passed away? What are you talking about?" This was a new one. "You ain't no closer to death than I am, buddy. You may be *further* from it for all I know."

Santini cocked his head as though he'd just been aroused by a new thought. "The reason behind losing my old identities, Edward—and there have been many of them—is that my essential identity is echoing me back."

"Santini," Animal said, wanting to change the subject, "you got something on your chin."

Santini snatched up his pillow, and in a violent motion, buried his head in it. "Gone?", he said, looking up.

"You bet."

Then Santini was off again, and as the overhead light cast a glow over the severity of his small, taut face, he said, "Before I forget this as well, Edward, let me explain. As a member of the Army OSS I was called upon to shuffle myself from identity to identity—a French Resistance fighter, an Italian partisan. I was there to watch Mussolini dragged with his mistress through the streets of Milan, and there when Hermann Göring's treasure was discovered. I played poker as a German agent, a British agent, a double agent, an American gentleman of means, all of them thoroughly researched so that I could actually feel their presence within me. A thoroughly disastrous position for a person like me whose own essential self is scattered at best. So you can see, Edward, I am no-man anymore, stripped of his past, now ready to engage upon a new journey into the future."

"Yeah, and what do you think you're gonna be in this future?"

"Free."

Animal took a slug from the bottle and set it on the floor. Santini barreled on.

"And, ironically enough, it all began the day I was killed in the fire in that Paris hotel."

What could he say? The guy died and here he was reborn.

"Whaddya think of headshrinkers, Santini?"

"Depends."

"On what?"

"Who they are."

"Whaddya think about goin' to one?"

"Emotionally?"

Animal shrugged. "Whatever."

"I'm not certain. And, by the way, I was also murdered by the SS. Twice."

"Twice?"

"That, Edward, is a remarkable accomplishment by any standards."

"I think that's pretty remarkable. We could play the Roxy, Santini, you and me. I could feed you lines—"

"And finally, I was castrated and put to death in a camp at Montauban."

"Listen. Santini. You ain't dead. Lemme be the first to give you the happy news. You're just a little crazy right now. You been through a lot. I prob'ly woulda acted the same way. But"—his finger went up—"it's time to . . . be . . . normal."

"Edward, may I interrupt you for a moment?"

"Be my guest."

"I have a confession to make."

"What is it?"

"I am not Michelangelo Santini."

Animal didn't know how much more he could take of this.

"Okay, who are you?"

"The original?"

"Why not."

"Jim Belasco. San Diego, California."

"Nice to meecha."

"Harriet and Jim Senior Belasco, a sister, Joan, and two dogs."

"Santini"—Animal felt himself creeping close to the edge—"if I was to tell you that you have—"

"I *am* Jim Belasco, Edward. Believe me. You must understand—I'm telling you this because in seven years with the OSS I have never had one friend, not one. My superiors in the service know my record. A few acquaintances along the way know pieces of my emotional self. I see you as a friend."

"Well, yuh know, Santini, I feel the same way."

"Thank you, Edward. I have had so many parts to play, I have lost the Jim Belasco that gave me life."

"Well, if you know that, what's the problem?"

"No problem. The OSS gave me many identities, some of whom were killed off. Those are the deaths I spoke of."

Animal waited to hear more.

"But some of me died with each of them."

"I can see that."

"And even when Jim Belasco died, though I didn't like him much, part of me died too."

"You *are* Jim Belasco . . . aren't you? Didn't you just—?"

"I *was* Jim Belasco. In fact he was the one who was castrated at Montauban."

Santini was drifting in and out now. His eyes were glazed over. His smile had a vacant, childlike curiosity to it, the kind that insane-asylum inmates carried around with them . . . Animal figured it was time.

"Okay, buddy," he said, standing up. "Snap out of it. We're going to bye-bye land."

"I'm so tired, Edward, so tired of all this."

"You bet, time for a little nappy-poo."

He helped Santini get dressed, combed his hair for him, and then, taking him gently by the arm, steered him down the corridor.

Their conversation on the way to sick bay was not a conversation but a monologue. Santini chattered away, telling Animal what good friends they were and what a pleasure it was to have finally made a friend, after all this time.

The surgeon took charge of him, and as he was being led away, Animal waved good-bye, wondering if Santini knew that he was now talking to someone else.

Nine bells sounded on deck, which meant an hour before the game resumed. Animal was sitting on the john reading an old *Saturday Evening Post* Kettle had given him, when Augie wandered in in his spiffy bathrobe and slippers.

"Hiya, handsome," Animal grinned, then swallowed whatever else he had to say because of the look on Augie's face, as if Augie were surprised to find him here.

"What's the matter?"

Augie sat down in the next stall and leaned forward so that he could face Animal.

"Nothing," he said.

"I hope so. That was no I-feel-like-a-million look you gave me there."

"I heard you and Santini last night."

"Did you hear when I hauled him off to sick bay? The poor guy finally flipped. Every day it was getting worse and worse until last night he went over the line."

"You think losing did it to him?"

"Yeah, but that was only the trigger. Just by bunking

with him it was obvious the problem started a long time ago. Anyway, the doc has him now."

"How long have you been sitting here, Pod?"

"Half hour or so, why?"

"You came here after taking Santini to sick bay?"

"No, I took him last night around one, went back to bed . . . What's with the questionnaire?"

"So you came here directly from your room?"

"Yeah."

Augie leaned back out of Animal's sight. "Interesting."

Animal had to leave the toilet seat to curve his head around the stall divider. "What's interesting?"

"Who do you think stole Santini's system?" Augie asked him.

"Stole his system? I don't know. I don't know if it *was* stolen. I'll tell you something: Santini was just weird enough to have lost it on purpose, knowing he'd have an excuse when he went bust. Furthermore, the fuckin' think was useless. Only a lunatic would steal that system, but being that Santini is the only lunatic I know of on this ship, I figure he must have been the thief. That's what I decided during those last wonderful days with the man."

"No," Augie said. "Somebody else stole it."

"Yeah? Who?"

"The same person who made sure Charlie Buck was taken out of the game—"

"Whoa! The Cowboy went overboard with twenty-three other guys, Eppy, remember?"

"All right, but you have to agree with me that Charlie, who was young and strong *and* not one to take chances— witness his poker—would not *take the chance* of going overboard. He would not put himself in the situation, unless he knew that he could handle it."

"So somebody pushed him?" Animal couldn't buy

Augie's idea about Charlie, but somebody else stealing Santini's system . . . ? Yeah, that was better than a fifty-fifty shot.

"What you have," he told Augie, "are two things that don't connect."

"Maybe." Augie pointed a finger. "First, let's consider the idea of somebody wanting to sabotage the game."

"Sabotage the game?" Animal got up and lumbered over to the shaving mirror where he took a second to admire his six-day-old beard. Gave him a kinda new, rugged look, he thought. To Augie's reflection in the mirror, he said, "You newspaper guys are too much. Everything's a mystery. Who would want to sabotage the game? There's no way *to* sabotage the game. The cards are clean. I ain't seen no signals thrown . . . that I know of. What do you know?"

"I know that something's going on."

"You got suspects, maybe?" Animal said, rolling his eyes.

"Maybe."

Just then Hubbard stumbled in half asleep, mumbling, "Good morning."

"Is this one of them?" Animal said.

"One of what?" Hubbard asked.

"Who the hell knows? I gotta feed the bird." With that Animal swaggered off down the corridor, Augie looking after him with a peculiar expression on his face.

Now that he didn't have a roommate any more, Animal could walk around naked, so he unwrapped the towel and stepped out of his boots and, walking barefoot to the seedbag, scooped out a handful. Turning toward the cage, he was surprised to find the poncho draped over it. He distinctly remembered uncovering it before going to the john.

"All right, kiddo," he said, yanking the cover away, "chow time."

It took Animal a good ten seconds to accept what he saw, and when he did, he threw up his breakfast. Hanging onto the cage for support, his feet spread apart, he dropped his head to his arms and peeked inside again.

Poncho's body was lying on the floor of the cage. Her head had been torn off, along with her legs, and the feathers spread about her on the floor like a funeral pyre. He saw one of her claws wrapped grotesquely over the bars, and her head, the beak's hard brown tongue crying out like a gargoyle, frozen in death.

Waiting for the nausea to subside he heard his name spoken and looked up to find Augie in the doorway, with Hubbard just behind him.

"You knew, didn't you, Eppy?" he managed to say.

Augie nodded solemnly. "Yeah. I saw it on my way in to the john."

Animal turned back to the cage, his voice barely audible. "You know how many times this bird saved my life? Thirteen . . . unlucky number. You know why Charlie Buck's luck ran out? He killed a bird, too, that seagull . . . and you know who else's luck has run cold-dead out . . . ? The guy who killed Poncho—I'm gonna find that sonofabitch. I'm gonna—"

Animal gave up trying to hold the tears back, and began to sob. Behind him, he could hear Augie say, "If there's anything you need . . ."

"Wait." Something occurred to him. "How much time before we play?"

Hubbard checked his watch. "Fifteen minutes."

Animal nodded without looking at them. "Deal me in."

First things first. Then he would get that fucker.

Chapter Eleven

ANIMAL'S MIND was boiling as he left the room. Why would anyone bother to kill a bird? Easy. To screw up his game. Or Hubbard might have wanted revenge because of the remarks he had made about his parents. Or Augie might have done it because he was such a violent bastard and tried to cover it up by taking him into his confidence. Even Santini might have eluded the doc and crept into the room when he had been in the john. To further complicate matters, any one of the two-hundred-whatever soldiers and crewmen might have engineered the act by bribing the sentry posted outside the players' quarters. There was a lot of outside money riding on this game.

He spotted the sentry. "*You* . . . yeah, you! You seen anybody pass by here in the last hour that shouldn't have been here?"

"No, sir, just authorized personnel."

"Meaning who?"

"You, Hubbard, Epstein. Chief Mate Murphy, Kettle, two mess boys, a guy from the laundry."

"Nobody else?"

"Nope," the sentry assured him.

"And you didn't leave your post during that time?"

"No, I didn't."

Animal put on a smile, though he didn't feel it. "Tell you what, I'll give you ten thousand dollars *right now* if you tell me the name of the man who bribed you to let him pass."

Animal could tell the sentry was thinking about *that,* but he couldn't tell if it was the money or the truth that was causing it. Ten thousand dollars oughta be enough to shake the facts out of anybody, bribed or not.

Finally, the sentry said, almost wistfully, "Well, sir, I sure wish I could oblige you 'cause that money sounds mighty nice . . . but, sorry, nobody's even offered me a dime."

"They haven't, huh?" Animal reached into his pocket and handed him a hundred-dollar bill, staring hard at him. "Here's somethin' for you, just in *case* you come up with somethin' later on . . . and there'll be more for you then. . . . See you, soldier." And he walked off.

When Animal came up on deck he felt dazed and exhausted—but up here everything seemed the same: soldiers talking over by the hatch; Kettle was passing out one of his mimeographed newsletters. Animal glanced at one: Staff Sergeant Joe Louis Barrow, heavyweight champ, had got divorced; writer Robert Benchley ("I've got to get out of these wet clothes and into a dry martini") had died at age fifty-six; Charles Lindbergh, on a technical mission to Paris, had said it wasn't like his heyday, 1927 ("I've been stopped on the street only once," he moaned); Johnny Desmond was still wowing

European audiences with "I'll Be Seeing You" and "Long Ago and Far Away."

Yeah, everything seemed the same. But Charlie Buck was dead, Santini was crazy—and now Poncho was dead. Someone was very definitely trying to screw them around. . . . He stuffed the newsletter in his pocket and waded through the troops without delivering his morning pep talk. Somehow he wasn't up to it today.

"How you feeling?" Augie asked when he sat down at the table.

"Like a million, and you?" Then he leaned closer to Augie. "Don't say nothin' about the bird, all right? Keep it under your hat."

He wished he could keep it out of his brain. He didn't feel ready to play right now. His body was at the table, but his mind was on Poncho. A pain the size of a basketball churned at the pit of his stomach, and he chewed furiously on a stick of gum to try to make it go away. Come *on*, he told himself, snap out of it. Whoever killed Poncho was going to get it and good, but for now he was damned if he was going to give the bastard the satisfaction of seeing him thrown off his game.

Animal got ready to play.

Kettle opened the money pouch while each man produced his slip of paper to match the one placed inside the pouch the night before. With Charlie gone his $145,000 remained in the ship's safe, which left $355,000 as the pot. No one knew who Charlie's relatives were or where they lived, so it was agreed the money would be given to his business manager, Major Tat, once the ship landed in New York.

The daily ritual began: fresh decks were broken out and passed around the table for each player's inspection, after which Kettle ripped off the seals and spread the cards face up on the table. The jokers were pulled out, ripped in two and deposited in Kettle's hat. If any deck proved unsatisfactory—which usually meant it didn't feel right in one of the player's hands—the cards were handed back to Kettle, who stacked the deck in five separate piles and ceremoniously ripped the piles in two, dumping them into the hat. These "dead" decks were left there throughout the day and then dumped overboard.

For the next few hours, the game was dull, a lot of players folding after the third and fourth cards, and betting low. The ante was raised to $2,000, but even that made no difference. With the game at a low ebb, they agreed to break for lunch around four-thirty. On their way out of the hold one of the soldiers sidled up to Animal and asked him if it was true that his bird had been knocked off.

"How'd you hear about that?"

"I don't know. That's the word."

"Forget it," Animal snapped. So the news was out.

Up in the officers' mess, Fumi served them lunch with his usual quiet formality, but before leaving stood at the entrance with a curious expression on his face.

"Excuse, please?"

"Yeah, what is it, Fumi?" Augie said.

"Canary?" Jesus, thought Augie, even Fumi knew. With a quick look at Animal, he answered, "All gone, Fumi."

"All gone?"

"Flew the coop, as they say," Animal replied, not looking up from his plate.

The comment appeared to be lost on Fumi.

"Went bye-bye, Fumi," Animal said irritably. "Just like you. Bye-bye, Fumi."

Augie held up his hand. "Wait a minute . . . Fumi, where's that cat of yours?"

"Oh, she down—"

Animal cut him off. "Forget it, Eppy. No cat did that." Then to Fumi, he added, more softly, "The bird died. You and your cat can say a little prayer for her, okay?"

Fumi finally understood and with an expression of profound remorse backstepped out.

They ate in silence, Animal picking at his food, until Hubbard could stand it no longer. He had been waiting patiently ever since that morning to hear more about what Animal and Augie had alluded to in the john, and finally he said, "I heard the word 'sabotage' mentioned today. Would either one of you care to elaborate on that?"

"Eppy has a theory," Animal said. "You wanna let him in on it?"

"You think I should?"

With a shrug and a quick glance at Hubbard, Animal said, "Why not?"

Augie repeated his notion about a link connecting the disasters to Santini, Charlie and Poncho.

"I haven't got any solid motives or suspects yet," he added. "But it's gone beyond coincidence. It could be one of the soldiers, you know. There's a lot of money floating around, a lot of money bet on each of us . . . I think we'd better be extra careful from now on: stay in our rooms, mix with them as little as possible . . . I already talked to Murphy and he's putting extra guards outside our quarters."

"What about prohibiting the troops from watching the game?" Hubbard suggested.

"Yeah," Animal said, "we could but what good would

it do? That's the safest place on the whole fuckin' ship, down there. And to tell the truth I kinda like the troops bein' up there in the bleachers, what with the noise and all that. But, lissen, if you two want 'em out, I'll go along."

They kicked the idea around for a while and finally agreed that the troops added to the game, and—Animal was right—it *was* the safest place. Not for a moment did anyone consider canceling the game.

After lunch, things began to take an interesting tack. In the morning, nobody had been winning or losing significantly. But now, suddenly, Augie started acting peculiarly. Not only had he begun losing heavily, he was playing such monumentally lousy poker that Hubbard took a moment to ask him if he felt all right.

"Yeah, I'm just a little out of whack with all this extracurricular garbage going on," Augie answered, but Hubbard did not entirely buy that. It was obvious that Augie's problem was lack of concentration: instead of paying attention to the cards Hubbard watched him drift off, watched him check and recheck his hole card as if he had forgotten what it was. Augie was sweating and seemed to be having difficulty breathing . . . There was definitely something more than "extracurricular garbage" on his mind.

By six o'clock Augie had dropped nearly half of his $145,000, most of it finding its way into Hubbard's pile.

The deal came around to Animal, who picked up the deck and offered the cut to Augie, then dealt the first card down, the second up, calling them out as he went: "In the words of our dear departed Cowboy, a Montana Whackback for the Captain." Which meant that Hubbard got a king. "And a double but for the dreamboat over here." An eight for Augie.

"All right," said Animal, dealing himself a three, "go ahead, Cap'n, bet the mighty one."

"Two thousand."

Augie called him.

"Up to me," said Animal. "Call, and raise you two back."

"On a pair of threes against my kings?" Hubbard said, matching the bet.

"That's two grand to me." Augie peeked at his hole card. "I'll call."

"Pot's right." Animal dealt the third card.

Hubbard caught a seven, Augie another eight. Animal a six, nothing there.

"Five thousand," Augie said.

"I'm in." Animal pushed in the bills.

Hubbard also called.

"Okay," said Animal, ready to deal number four. "Here yuh go, Cap'n, sir. Hey, lookee here, two sevens. Now for Augie Doggie . . . Augie? Hey, you all right?"

Augie's head had drifted off to the side, his face constricted in pain. He felt as if a war had begun in his stomach. After a moment, the spasms receded.

"I'm okay," he said, shaking it off. "Deal."

Animal turned a five for Augie and a four for himself, giving him the possibility of an outside straight.

"Your pair of eights are still high, Eppy," Animal said. "Whaddya going to do?"

Augie was having great difficulty doing anything at all at the moment, let alone keeping his mind on the game. With a perfunctory glance at Hubbard's pair of sevens and Animal's mishmash he used both hands to count out his bills.

"I'll bet five thousand," he said.

"I won't." Animal folded his cards.

Just then Augie let out a groan and doubled over.

From a distance, he heard the soldiers starting to murmur and Hubbard telling Kettle to get the doctor and then saw him kneeling down, using a handkerchief to wipe his brow.

"What'samatter, Eppy?" Animal said. "Gas?"

It took a moment for him to answer. "Gas," he said, nodding. "Must be gas, cramps or something. I'll be fine."

Except to Hubbard and Animal and everybody else in the hold he didn't look fine. Sweat was pouring out of him, his eyes had glazed over and his skin had taken on the color of paste.

Once again the pains receded and Augie, who had no idea what was happening, pushed himself back in the chair and took a long, deep breath.

"I might have to take a break pretty soon," he said, "but first let's finish the hand."

"You're sure?" Animal said.

"Yeah."

Hubbard slipped back to his seat and Animal gave a recap: "All right. Eppy bet five grand on the eights. It's up to you, Cap'n."

Hubbard took another of his long moments to analyze the situation. Augie had not raised in the beginning, which meant . . . which meant what? Considering Augie's frame of mind Hubbard had no idea what it meant. Chances were he had no more than the eights, maybe with a picture card in the hole. On the other hand, Augie might have been suckering him in and actually *did* have the third eight in the hole. After all, he had been very anxious, pain and everything, to continue the hand.

Hubbard took the safe route.

"I'll call," he said, peeling off the bills.

"All righty," Animal announced, "last card coming. Holy Fuck, Cap'n! Three big sevens! And . . . Holy Fuck, again! Eights and fives for the Ep! Three sevens beats the two pair, Cap'n. You're up."

"Check," Hubbard said, giving the ball to Augie.

When there was no response, Animal leaned over to his left and said, "Hey, Eppy! Check to you. You with us?"

The needles had started crawling back inside Augie's stomach, and to make things worse an army of pounding hammers had begun invading his brain. He took off his dark glasses and laid them on the table, then took a couple of deep breaths, which was no help. The game was fading in and out, and it wasn't until Animal screamed at him again that he realized that it was his move.

He took a look at his hole card to reconfirm that he had the full-house, eights over fives, and then tried to focus on Hubbard's hand, but his cards seemed so damn far away.

"What have you got there, Hubbard?"

"Three sevens."

"Three sevens, right." He had them beat, no problem there. Logically—and it was becoming increasingly more difficult for him to think in those terms—he should bet just enough to tempt Hubbard to call him. After all, Hubbard could have his own sevens and kings full and might pay to see Augie's winning hand.

"Ten thousand dollars," Augie said.

Animal swung toward Hubbard. "Ten grand to you, Cap'n."

It appeared as if Hubbard were concentrating on Augie's cards, but he was not. He was counting Augie's money.

"About fifty thousand?" he said to Augie.

Augie didn't seem to hear him, so he repeated it. Like an old man, Augie rotated his head and body all at once until he faced Hubbard squarely.

"What's that?" he said in a dry, raspy voice.

"The cash you have. Does it come to about fifty thousand?"

"I'm not sure." He looked down at his pile and back at Hubbard. "Why?"

"I'll call your ten thousand and raise you what you have left."

Augie was sure he hadn't hear him correctly until the noise from the spectators told him otherwise. Minutes seemed to pass before he heard Animal saying, ". . . the money, Eppy, how much you got there?"

The stack of bills felt like lead in his hand.

"Why don't we postpone this till you feel better, Eppy," Animal started to say. "Maybe in—"

"I'm in for whatever it is!" Augie blurted out, suddenly angry. He slammed the bills on the table and said, "Count it!"

Animal picked up the bills and held them out so Augie could watch what he was doing.

"You see me?"

Augie waved him off. "Whatever it is, I believe you."

"You sure you don't—"

"Count the fucking money!"

Animal ran through it twice and announced the figure: "Fifty-one thousand, two hundred."

"I'm in."

Without waiting for Hubbard to turn over his cards, Augie carefully reached for his hole card and flipped over the third eight, not even bothering to look, he was feeling so crummy.

"Do me a favor, Pod, would you, and rake in the dough for me? I don't feel worth a shit."

Animal didn't say anything for a few seconds.

"Pod?" Augie said, his hand over his eyes.

"What?"

"Did you do it?"

"No."

"No? C'mon, be a sport, rake it in for me, huh?"

"I'd like to, Eppy, but Hubbard has four sevens."

When he heard that, Augie spun so violently he knocked over both coffee cups and clipped Animal on the arm as he went by. Forgetting his stomach for the moment he fixed his eyes on the sevens but still couldn't understand exactly what had happened, what the sevens meant. He knew he had lost the hand but what he did not realize for another few seconds was that he had gone bust, was out of money, finished.

The stomach pains thundered back more furiously than ever; he let out a cry that sounded like strangulation and vomited.

Animal was there to catch him when he toppled off his chair. A sentry moved over to help Hubbard spread a blanket so that Animal could ease Augie onto it and drape a trenchcoat over him.

The surgeon followed Kettle into the hold and made a perfunctory scan: pulse, eyes, heart, throat.

"What a helluva time to get seasick," Animal said.

The doctor probed around a while longer. "Looks more like food poisoning to me."

Food poisoning? The words echoed through the hold. If Epstein had it a lot of other guys must: they all ate the same chow, didn't they? A few of them began feeling uneasy sensations in their stomachs.

Two medical aides hustled in with a stretcher and strapped Augie in, then, after the doctor gave them instructions, carried the body to sick bay where the doctor would pump his stomach.

After they had gone and Animal and Hubbard were back in their seats, Animal said, "How *you* feelin', Cap'n?"

"I'm feeling all right. You?"

"I ain't sick but I'm pretty goddamn suspicious, if you wanna know the truth." He leaned forward and said so that the troops couldn't hear, "What say we call it a night and start up again in the morning, you for that?"

"Sure."

"Unless you wanna take what we have right now and call it quits."

"I'd rather play it out."

"You would, huh?"

"Yes."

"Yeah," said Animal, "me, too."

But as he said it he felt a twinge of fear. Charlie. Santini. Poncho. Epstein. Now there were only two left.

But god*damn* if he was going to quit.

In his seat, Hubbard was thinking the same thing. Only two players to go. And $355,000 between them.

They exchanged a glance. Correction: $355,000 for *one* of them.

Chapter Twelve

"Eppy, you look dead!"

Animal was genuinely shocked when he entered sick bay and saw Augie. Epstein had turned the color of granite, and the lines in his face, like black canals, made him look ten years older. The doctor told him that food poisoning followed by dehydration produces that effect and that, considering the dosage, Augie was very fortunate to be alive and, from the looks of things, Animal could believe it. The doctor also told him that Augie's stomach had been pumped to capacity but that something had gone wrong with his vocal cords and he wasn't able to speak very well, so he shouldn't spend too much time with him.

Animal dragged a stool over to Augie's berth. "I mean it, Eppy, you look terrible. That's what they call reverse psychology, it's supposed to make you feel better. The doc said you wanted to see me. What's up?"

Augie gave no indication that he had heard a thing, so Animal craned his neck over him and stared directly into his face. Augie's lips were moving slightly but no sound was coming out.

"Talk up," Animal said to him. "I can't hear you."

"Fig . . . figu . . . figured it out."

"Figured it out? Yeah. What? You figured what out?" Eppy, don't go away. You figured out what?

"Edward?" Animal turned and saw Santini down the aisle waving to him.

"Hiya, buddy," he called back. "I'll be down to see you in a minute."

What with Santini and now Augie, both looking like death warmed over, Animal got the uneasy feeling that one of these sickbeds had his own name written on it.

He lowered his head down to Augie again so that his ear was just an inch or so above his mouth. "Go ahead," he said, "I'm listenin'."

"Plan."

"Plan. Right." He waited. "What plan? *Whose* plan? Gimme a name."

But all he could feel was Augie's faint breath.

"Eppy, don't leave me now. C'mon." He looked to see if the doctor was watching and then gently slapped Augie's cheek. "C'mon kid, snap out of it. You figured out the plan, so who's behind it? C'mon. Gimme the name!"

Animal waited until it looked as if Augie wasn't about to say anything else, and in fact as if he had stopped breathing.

"Doc!" he screamed, and the surgeon rushed over with an oxygen tank.

"He's still with us?" Animal asked him as he lowered a plastic cup over Augie's mouth.

"Yes, but that'll be it for today."

"How long before he comes to?"

"Tomorrow perhaps."

"I don't know if I got that long," Animal mumbled

and, thanking the doctor, went over to visit Santini who was sitting up in bed, looking a little better than last time.

"Hiya doin?" Animal said, patting him on the shoulder. "What's the good word?"

"I was just thinking of Azrael," he said with a smile.

"Who?"

"The bright angel of death. I've been formulating my own autobiographical necrology. As a matter of fact here,"—he handed Animal a sheet of paper—"you can see for yourself."

On the paper was a series of stick figures, one broken in two, another hanging, one consumed by fire, another holding a penis and genitals in its hand. Above each figure was a word defining the method of execution.

"All me," Santini said with childlike reverie. "All gone."

"Yeah, they're real . . . nice, Santini. Real nice. Ah . . . well, listen, buddy, I gotta go tune up for the showdown with Hubbard, you know? So, take care of yourself."

"Okay, Edward. Viva Azrael!"

"Sure thing."

On his way out Animal felt like throwing up.

Animal's tune-up consisted of a bottle of Scotch he had wheedled out of Kettle, which he carried up to his room, set next to a glass and a bowl of ice, and proceeded to kill.

The more he drank, the faster his thoughts came, and the faster they came, the more complex the puzzle grew. Okay, first things first: who was responsible for what? Nobody was responsible for Santini going off the deep end but Santini himself, he was sure of that. He was also ready to buy Augie's theory that Charlie Buck had been pushed overboard, though he knew it would be impossible to prove.

And Poncho? He didn't even want to think about that. After burying the bird at sea that night, he was considering getting rid of everything that even reminded him of her. He looked over the cage sitting beside him on the footlocker while two years of memories flooded through him—then he swung his right leg over and blasted the thing against the bulkhead.

He knew he had to get his mind off Poncho, otherwise it was going to drive him nuts, so he shifted over to Augie's mysterious sickness. He couldn't help wondering if he might have gotten sick, too, if he had eaten lunch, but he'd been so screwed up over Poncho's death he'd sent the food back to the galley. After Augie's attack, he had managed to ask Kettle to take the food down to the doc to have it checked out—except that it had been dumped. And the plates had been washed, so there was no way to have them inspected. No trace of anything. Very neat, he thought, too neat.

Then, about two-thirds of his way into the bottle, something hit him hard enough for him to leap off the bed and, taking the bottle with him, run out the door.

"You busy?"

Hubbard looked up from his book and said, "No, come on in."

Animal swaggered over to Augie's old bunk and balanced himself against the stanchion.

"You like some of this?" he said, holding up the bottle.

"No, thanks."

"Yeah, that's right. You don't drink, do you, Captain?" he said in a nasty tone.

"On occasion."

Hubbard couldn't tell whether Animal was leading up to something or just being disagreeable, but he was definitely unfriendly, and drunk. He watched him take a healthy slug from the bottle and place it on the foot-locker.

"You know, Captain," Animal began with a boozy, philosophical intonation, "I was just sitting over there next door minding my own business when all of a sudden I got this weird idea, which I thought I would come over here and share with you."

He took a second to get his thoughts in order. "Do you realize that all these strange things that been happenin' to us ain't been happenin' to *all* of us?"

"What do you mean?"

"Just what I said. Every one of us has been fucked over at least once . . . everyone, that is, except you. You ain't been fucked over, Captain. Why is that?"

"I don't know."

"C'mon, Cap'n, you can level with me."

"What are you insinuating?"

"I ain't insinuating nothin'. I'm tellin' you straight out." Animal was heating up. "Santini's system . . . the Cowboy overboard . . . my bird . . . Eppy with the poison . . . and you—nothin'! I want an answer, Hubbard, and now."

"Look, Podberoski," Hubbard said as calmly as he could, "my turn just hasn't come, that's all. Epstein's didn't come till this afternoon."

"You got it all figured out, doncha? That's what you are, Captain, slick, greased lightning . . . mind like a whip." He shook his head. "Wrong. You *think* you're hot shit—silver bars on the shoulders—old man's a general —lotta dough in your pocket. Evan Hubbard the Fourth. King Louie the Fourteenth. *Big fuckin' deal.* And you know what else I figured out? I'm the only one you couldn't get to. Kill my bird? Sure, it ruined me for a while, but I'm known for one thing, Cap'n—I bounce back . . . and I *don't* scare easy!"

"I'll take you up on your offer of a drink—"

"The hell you will! You're lucky I don't break this bottle across your face!"

He took a menacing step in Hubbard's direction and then suddenly broke out with a big smile. "Scared you there for a second, eh?"

Hubbard wasn't laughing. What the hell was this?

"Yeah," he admitted, "you had me scared."

Animal's face darkened again. "Well that's just the *preview*, Captain. Tomorrow we got the main event, at which, out of the goodness of my heart, and with all intents of destroying your ass, I'm gonna let you suffer for a while first, put you through torture you never seen. You think Santini's out of whack? *Wait.* By the time I get done with you they'll be able to string a rope between your ears."

Animal pointed a finger at Hubbard and said very seriously, "I'm convinced that you got something to do with this sabotage. Process of elimination, you're the only one left. However, you may not be the only one in on it." He had more to say but let it pass because with all the talking, the thinking and the booze he was getting tired and wanted to go to sleep. Plus he was slurring his words, a warning that his argument was starting to break down.

He walked unsteadily to the door, turned sideways to Hubbard, and with a crooked, upturned smile, muttered, "Good night, Captain."

With that he disappeared, whistling.

When Animal got back to his room he finished off the bottle of Scotch and fell asleep with his clothes on.

Around three he was awakened by a noise that sounded like pipes tapping overhead, but he was too out of it to pay much attention and went back to sleep. A few minutes later the noise started up again, but louder. Annoyed, he tried to muffle it by pulling the pillow over his head, but the goddamn sound got so irritating he threw the pillow on the floor and swung his legs over the bunk, looking for something to heave at it. The tapping stopped . . .

. . . and started again. Now that Animal was fairly awake he began to realize there was something peculiar about that noise. He'd never heard pipes knock like that before . . . it sounded as if *somebody* was doing it with a wrench or something—the same somebody who was trying to sabotage the game. Hubbard? He pulled out a bottle of apc's and washed them down with sink water to get rid of his splitting headache, wrapped his trenchcoat around him and crept down the corridor to Hubbard's room. The sonofabitch was sleeping like a baby. Yeah, but he still could have done the tapping, run back and slipped under the covers . . .

He continued on down the corridor to talk to the sentry. The sentry knew less than he did about the noise so he dragged him back to the room for a listen. They listened for thirty minutes, but no tapping.

"I'm not just makin' this up," Animal said. "I heard it."

"I believe you."

"What's up there?" he said, pointing to the ceiling.

"I don't know."

Animal debated going for a look, but could barely keep his eyes open.

"Look . . . I *gotta* get some sleep so I'll be in Charlie Buck's old room if anybody wants me."

Animal hauled his bedclothes to Charlie's room, crawled under them, and was asleep in minutes.

A few minutes later he was awakened by the tapping of pipes.

Chapter Thirteen

THE MORNING DAWNED BRIGHT and clear—the first sunlight any of them had seen since leaving Europe—and a new electricity crackled among the men milling around Number 1 hatch waiting for Animal and Hubbard to show. This was it: D-Day. The showdown. No one doubted the game would come to an end today—one way or another.

Though the temperature was just below forty, overcoats and some shirts had been shed, and the barechested among them sauntered around extolling the virtues of a tan, while the big bettors huddled with the bookmakers looking for the best odds they could get—there was no doubt Hubbard was the favorite. The morning line had him three to one based on his consistency, yesterday's play—and the fact that he was entering the game with nearly twice as much money as Animal.

The first player to appear was Hubbard himself, marching down the deck with his long, lanky stride, the sun beating down on his blond hair, his pressed, starched khakis rustling . . . and a set of captain's bars gleaming off his shoulders. The men stopped what they were doing —this was the first time any of them had seen Hubbard in full regalia and by this time most of them had even forgotten he was an officer—and watched. He seemed different somehow, icier, more formal. The air grew quiet.

Hubbard stepped along, stopping just short of the foremast, and let his eyes roam slowly through the crowd. Then, with a grin, he said: "What's the matter with you guys? This some kind of a wake?"

With a swell of laughter, the tension broke, and the troops surrounded him, cracking about his uniform and pressing him to say something about the game.

"Come on, Captain, what's the word?"

"Well, I'll tell you, gentlemen, you know I'm not a betting man"—more laughter—"but if I *were,* I'd bet the whole bundle on myself!"

Cameras clicked away, the soldiers asked him to pose this way and that, with his cap on and off, standing against the uptakes or with his back to the rail, staring out to sea or into the camera.

Hubbard was happy to oblige; it made him feel like a celebrity, which in a way he was. It wasn't every day a guy got to play in a half-million-dollar poker game, much less find himself in the lead down the stretch. Casablanca, the British Major, the specter of the General . . . they all seemed so far away now.

He had gotten the idea for the full uniform just this morning—it seemed appropriate, on this final day, to dress for the occasion. And besides, it might rankle Podberoski, if that were possible . . .

He spotted Kettle and his armed guard climbing down the ladder from the bridge and, like some crack drill squad, march across the deck, all spit-shined and

Brassoed, with Kettle throwing him a salute. It looked like everyone had the same idea.

"Captain Hubbard," Kettle barked out, holding the salute.

He returned it and said, "Good morning, Mister Kettle. Lovely morning, isn't it?"

"Yessir. Jest perfect."

The troops opened a wedge for Kettle's entourage as it moved briskly through and vanished into the hold. Some of the men asked Hubbard if he would mind waiting around so that they could get pictures of him and Animal together. Hubbard was just saying he really should be getting down—when Animal appeared.

The reactions ranged from shock to plain disbelief. On their best day, Animal's fatigues looked like something the cat dragged in, but now the pants had sharp creases in them, the sun glistened off his belt buckle, his boots were bloused and wore the kind of shine a man could shave in, and—the real shocker—Animal's cherished week-old beard, which he had sworn he wouldn't shave off till the game was over, was gone. *Nobody* was going to top Animal in a game of Intimidation Poker.

Except that neither the uniform nor his boots nor his beardless face could hide the fact that he was in very bad shape. The tip-off was in his eyes: red-rimmed, tugged down at the edges, as full of red lines as a road map. They had just enough life left in them to let him see where he was going.

Animal had figured out that morning that he had gotten maybe two hours sleep last night. The tapping noise had stopped around six A.M., but by that time he was so close to the game he couldn't sleep anyway. But he was damned if he was going to let Hubbard have the satisfaction of knowing that.

"Cap'n," he said, walking up to Hubbard. "This has got to be . . . Well, *excuse* me for living. These captain bars of yours . . . Trying to put the pressure on me?"

He moved past Hubbard and with renewed energy addressed the troops. "Fellas, whaddya think of this, eh? Seven days I ain't seen his bars. Today? He's pullin' rank. *But do we care?*"

"No!" they shouted, showing once again who the personal favorite was, even if the betting was going the other way. Animal acknowledged the response, raising his arms in a victory stance.

"How 'bout getting the two of you?"

Animal hammed it up: getting up on his tiptoes and kissing Hubbard on the cheek, making faces, doing Barrymore impressions. He was beginning to wake up . . . This photography session was good for him.

"Hey, Hubbard, what do you think about getting a dealer? There's only the two of us now."

"A dealer? Who?"

"What about Kettle?"

The answer arrived a little too quickly for Hubbard. "Why him?" he asked.

"He's on the inside. I don't think he can fool with the cards, do you?"

"I don't know . . ."

Animal pressed it. "I don't like the idea of passing the deal back and forth. It's a pain in the ass and it's not the way it should be done. You don't like Kettle? Name somebody."

Hubbard reluctantly agreed . . . Passing the deal would be an unnecessary burden and Kettle was a logical choice . . . "I suppose you've already got his consent?"

"Yeah, at breakfast," Animal told him. "He'll probably be a little nervous at first but he's played cards before and he's been watchin' us for the last week. So if he don't work out we get rid of him."

"All right," Hubbard said. "I'll give it a shot."

"Attaboy." Animal wheeled around to face the troops. "No more pictures, fellas. Wait till the break."

This was likely to be their last visit to The Tomb—a not at all unpleasant thought for either of them—but even The Tomb was fixed up today. With no rain last night Kettle had been able to leave the hatch cover off, giving the hold its first breath of air all week, and the clean-up crew had apparently worked overtime: not only had the hold been swept and washed down but the table and chairs waxed and buffed to a high polish. There was even music blaring over a high-powered ship-to-shore radio Kettle had brought in—American stations out of New York and Baltimore, now that the *John Logan* had pulled within range.

Kettle was delighted when Animal told him Hubbard had agreed to his deal: it was the true capstone to his trip. "You can depend on me, sir."

Once more the fresh decks were broken out, each player inspecting them for the tell-tale odor of a hot iron or a tampered seal, and the money pouch unlocked, Animal and Hubbard producing their slips of paper to match the ones within.

$355,000, in $100, $500 and $1,000 bills were stacked side by side on the table, then each man spent a few moments counting out his money: Hubbard's $230,000 against Animal's $125,000. Kettle provided them with rubber bands to wrap around stacks of $5,000 each, while Animal, feeling himself lapse back into bleary-eyed fatigue, ordered the messboys to keep his coffee cup filled and watched Hubbard sitting straight as a pin across from him, peeling off his money with the crisp, precise hands of a surgeon.

"What made you decide to shave?" Hubbard asked him without looking up.

"Had a nightmare—that underneath the beard my face was gone. I hadda find out."

"You look tired."

"How sharp of you to notice."

Hubbard finished his count and nodded to Kettle, who motioned for the guard to let the troops into the hold.

One by one, they swarmed down the ladder and fanned out, scrambling for the best seats, talking and whistling along with the tune on Kettle's radio. With everybody saving seats for everybody else arguments broke out but were immediately squelched—Kettle, as sergeant-at-arms, had already banned a couple dozen guys from watching the game. The bookmakers took their final bets and sat together in a private section, pockets bulging with money, protected by their own cadre of guards.

Kettle turned the radio off and called for silence, then parked himself in what used to be Charlie Buck's seat.

He practiced shuffling for a while and then dealt a few rounds while Hubbard and Animal watched carefully that he kept the deck down and didn't expose the bottom card. They could tell right off that he wasn't a beginner by the way the cards slid off the deck and landed where he aimed them. Of course, he wasn't nearly as good as Hubbard, out of whose beefy hands the cards had sailed like sheets of rain, or Animal who had snap-spinned them off the deck, but Kettle was competent, a good amateur, and after he dealt a dozen hands or so they told him they were ready.

"Gentlemen," he said, pumping authority into his

Kentucky accent, "this is five-card stud, with all the rules still applying. Agreed?"

They agreed and each anted up $2,000 while Kettle shuffled six times, three times for each man, and slapped the deck down in front of Animal, who tapped it and said, "They're good."

Kettle ran the down cards and turned the seconds up, calling them out: "Seven of diamonds for Captain Hubbard and king of hearts for Mister Podberoski. The king bets."

"Thousand."

"Call," Hubbard said, matching it.

"Pot's right," Kettle intoned. "Third card. Nine of clubs for Captain Hubbard and an ace of hearts for Mister Podberoski. Ace high bets."

Animal let his eyes drift across the table and back.

"Five grand on the bullet," he said, pitching a rubber-band stack into the center.

"I'll call your five thousand," Hubbard said, "and raise you five more."

There was a quick burst of noise from the gallery which faded to silence as Animal lit up his cigar.

"Well, now," he said, smiling conspicuously, "and I was about to die of boredom. Okay, Cap'n, see your five and raise it another ten."

Counting the ante, Hubbard's investment was already at $13,000. Animal's bet meant one of two things: either Podberoski was pushing the bluff or he had the case ace.

Hubbard said in an even voice, "I'll call," and pushed the stacks in.

"Run 'em, Red," Animal said to Kettle, who picked up the deck and dealt the fourth card: a diamond deuce for Hubbard and a diamond nine for Animal.

The hands thus far:

HUBBARD	ANIMAL
9 hearts (hole)	5 clubs (hole)
7 diamonds	K hearts
9 clubs	A hearts
2 diamonds	9 diamonds

"Ace is still high, Mister Podberoski," Kettle said.

"Twenty thousand dollars," Animal said, casually pushing the bills into the center.

It was a mystery to no one that the best Hubbard could have was two nines, which, considering the way Animal was betting, was a loser . . . that is, if—a $20,000 "if" to Hubbard—Animal wasn't bluffing.

Animal, meanwhile, with the advantage of knowing Hubbard's best possible hand, had made his mind up to run with this hand to the end. It became a matter of putting himself into a kind of trance; he actually convinced himself that he *did* have the aces, a conviction he hoped would show through to Hubbard and chase him the hell out.

Hubbard had been watching Animal closely, listening for modulations in his voice and looking to see if he rubbed his fingers together as he had done on previous bluffs. But of course with Podberoski you never knew if he was throwing off phony signals or not. Without the beard, it was like playing against a completely different person, which Hubbard figured was the reason he *had* shaved it off. His face was pink and chubbier and he looked younger without the hair, less sinister somehow.

But none of that made any difference to Hubbard at the moment because he had no idea if Podberoski had his aces or not, and he wasn't about to pay $20,000 to find out.

"I'm out," he said, turning over his cards.

Animal let out an exaggerated sigh of relief and scooped in the pot. "Now, that," he said, peering at

Hubbard from under his Faustian eyebrows, "is poker."

The hold was heating up again so Animal made a big deal out of taking off his shirt, unbuttoning his trousers and, with a big sweeping gesture, relighting his cigar.

"You interested in knowin' what beat you, Cap'n?"

"If you'd like to show me."

"How much is it worth to you?"

"Nothing."

"I'll sell you a look for a hundred bucks."

Hubbard laughed. "I just paid you thirteen thousand."

"True, true. In which case"—he boxed his cards and buried them in the deck—"why bother? I *had* the second ace; let it be a lesson to yuh."

For the next few hours it was a seesaw duel, tight and unremarkable, with one long stretch of no-stay and the rest third and fourth card folds.

This was the time when the pure art and steel nerves of poker-playing made their mark on the game, when the subtlety and refinement probably lost on the gallery ruled that sacred territory Animal called "the soul of the game."

In that territory nothing mattered but the next turn of the card and the expression on the opponent's face. It was in-fighting, close to the bone, where the tiniest wrong move could be picked up and turned into a major weapon. Santini had called this time "purgatory," when all the sins and strategies of the past come forth in judgment, to send you up or drive you down. Low pairs won here, and no pairs, and if a powerhouse happened to show up on one side of the table or the other, it never made it past the third card.

For Hubbard it was like grinding out yardage, working the clock, wearing down the opposition, and regardless of the way it looked from the bleachers, one hell of a lot of money changed hands. Confidence turned into fear. Guys hanging on to their last buck could make comebacks in this kind of game that were remarkable things to see.

But there was no comeback in Animal's cards, just the reverse. The cards were really doing a job on him. When he caught a pair of sevens, Hubbard had eights. He'd have a flush working and Hubbard would suddenly pair up with kings. Little by little he watched his hundred and sixty thousand bucks drop to ninety-four.

Something had to happen, so at seven he called for the dinner break.

They left the guards to protect their money and followed Kettle up the ladders to the officers' mess where the three of them fed on steak, rice and canned vegetables, a bottle of Bordeaux and a pie of Fumi's creation which he identified as lemon meringue. It wasn't even close.

As they had done at breakfast, Animal and Hubbard took the precaution of waiting for the cook to taste their food before eating it themselves. Nobody wanted a repetition of Augie's collapse.

"This wine is very good, Mister Kettle," said Hubbard.

"Thank you, Captain."

"Yeah, and I think Captain Hubbard will agree with me," Animal added, "that you're doin' real good with the cards, right, Cap'n?"

"Very well indeed."

"Thank you, fellas," Kettle smiled, honored by their praise. "I'm doin' the best I can, trying not to slow things up or anything."

"No, no, doin' just fine," Animal told him, stabbing a piece of steak.

Flattered that he'd been asked to dine with them, Kettle decided to strike up a conversation. "What do you fellas plan on doing once you get home, if you don't mind me askin'?"

"If I lose I'm going to kill myself, that's one thing," Animal said. "Other than that I'm gonna get married. To Mildred Memory, a terrific dame."

"Memory?" Hubbard asked. "That's her name?"

"I tried to get her to change it. She said, okay, marry me. I figured if I could make it through the war, Mildred would be a cinch. I just don't know about her kids."

"Her kids?"

"She got married while I was away, husband took off or somethin'. I ain't got all the details, except for the two kids. Six years is a long time to wait."

"Yes, it is."

"So I figured if she couldn't wait, neither could I. Did my share of humpin' over there. Wops, froggies, the Kraut broads, hairy armpits and all. Now I'm ready to settle down. I'm gonna be thirty-five next year. It's about time, right?"

"I suppose," Hubbard said.

"Yeah, and how 'bout you, Cap'n, you married?"

"I was."

"No kidding? What happened?"

"It didn't work out."

"Oh."

They continued eating in silence and every once in a while Animal peeked up from his food at Hubbard, wondering what kind of woman he would be married to, probably some society dame with frilly dresses and blonde hair like his own, a Southern belle dripping with culture, just the kind of woman that turned Animal off.

"What was she like, Cap'n . . . your wife, what was she like?"

Animal was surprised by the way Hubbard rattled off the description: "Tall. Dark-haired. Thin. Very attrac-

tive. Smart. Ambitious. More situational than concept-
ual."

"More what than what?"

"More interested in things than ideas . . . what someone *does,* not what someone is." Hubbard took a bite.
"She's really very bright but not intelligent, you know . . .
Stored up volumes of information but doesn't know what
to do with it. An emotional desert."

Animal heard no bitterness in his voice, or anything
else, for that matter. He could have been talking about a
plant for all the emotion he put into it. Kind of a desert
himself, he thought.

"Yeah, but did you like her?" Animal asked.

"I'm attracted to that type of woman."

"Uh huh. You like women, do yuh?"

Hubbard waited a second before answering. "Not
really," he said. "No."

No doubt about it, Animal thought, Hubbard was a
very strange guy, rich and proper like the hotsy-totsy
Yale kids that used to come into Brooklyn sometimes
and visit Ridnauer down the block. He used to hate
those Yale kids, the phony fucking sonofabitches, just
like he was really starting to hate Hubbard right now.
Plus the asshole didn't like women. It would be a pleasure
beating him.

"Women probably don't like you either, Cap'n," he
said. "You ready to play cards, let's go."

Upon Animal's request, Kettle located a GI who said
he gave rubdowns and also had eyedrops and mouthwash sent up from sick bay. Before going back into The
Tomb, Animal and Hubbard showered, shaved and
changed their clothes, and had a massage, and by the
time they returned to the table they were refreshed and
ready to go.

Kettle broke open a fresh deck, passed it around and cracked his knuckles, preparing for the deal.

"You ready, gentlemen?"

They were and, taking up the deck, Kettle offered the cut to Animal and ran them.

They played more of the same for the next couple of hours, more no-stays and third and fourth card folds. During this time Animal drank two full pots of coffee by himself and used the mouthwash to kill the foul taste on his gums. He had taken off his shirt and loosened his belt again and used up a half dozen damp washcloths on his face and arms—he found it incredible that no more than a ripple of perspiration ever showed on Hubbard's forehead. The man played like ice, speaking only to check and raise and ask the messboys for glasses of water.

Kettle dealt hand after hand, calling out the cards and the bets, laying the deck down and resting his elbows on the table. They passed the normal ten o'clock deadline and pushed into the early morning hours because, according to Murphy, the *John Logan* would pull into New York late the next afternoon.

At about two A.M. Kettle dealt a hand that started out like a lot of the others.

After the hole cards Kettle turned a heart seven to Hubbard and spade eight to Animal, who bet $1,000. Hubbard called him and Kettle dealt the next card, a heart six to Hubbard and spade seven to Animal.

Animal took a look at Hubbard's six and seven of hearts and his own seven and eight of spades and figured it just might be the right time to throw a scare into the captain.

"Well now," he said, stretching his arms out behind him. "Looks like we got a couple of hot possibilities goin' here." With his spade nine in the hole he had the slim makings of a flush but what he wanted Hubbard to figure was a pair of sevens, so he bet them like he had them.

"Ten thousand dollars," he said, pushing the money in.

Hubbard didn't believe he had the sevens and called him.

"Fourth card coming," Kettle announced. "Five of hearts for Captain Hubbard, straight flush working and" —he turned Animal's—"a spade six, with a straight flush over here, too. Bet the eight-high, Mister Podberoski."

Animal had to think about this for a second. His own eight-high spades on the board beat Hubbard's seven-high hearts. A big bet, he figured, might chase the captain out, maybe not. A small bet would be like pissing in the wind.

"Your bet, Mister Podberoski," Kettle said.

"I know!" he snapped.

He counted up the money already in the pot—$26,000. He counted his own money—seventy-five grand and change—against Hubbard's $250,000. Just for a second he tried to visualize what Hubbard held, tried to get a mental picture of it and how he would respond to a big bet if he were in Hubbard's position. Hubbard could afford to chase him with so much cash, but would he? The problem with a big bet was that Hubbard might have a high card in the hole—a winner at this point. Another problem was wondering just how much he was giving away by doing all this thinking: Hubbard could be reading him like a book.

He took an eraser to his brain and said, "I'll check to the power."

"Check to you, Captain Hubbard," Kettle intoned.

Hubbard leaned back in his chair, folding one hand over his chest and rubbing his forehead with the other. Then he floated one hand down to the stacks of $5,000 with the rubber bands around them and fingered them until he had six.

"That'll be thirty thousand dollars," he said, edging the money in.

The spectators—those that were left—made some noise, but Kettle stopped it by a simple turn of the head.

Animal did not move. He dropped his eyes from Hubbard's face to his own 6-7-8 of spades and then across the table to Hubbard's 5-6-7 of hearts. He felt a shiver start at the small of his back and race up his spine and down his right arm; picking up his cigar, he lit it quickly, shaking the match and flipping it into the ashtray.

What the fuck was going on here? Had Hubbard paired up? Was he working on the come? Hubbard had taken time to make his bet, but that meant nothing because he always took time.

The tension was building way too fast for him so he figured he'd better break it up, and said with a half-smile, "Whaddya got, pair of kings?"

"Three of them," Hubbard answered with no expression whatever.

Animal left the cigar in his mouth, biting down hard on it and flicking the end with his tongue. Thirty thousand. What could he do? With a straight flush working he couldn't fold, especially when he had Hubbard beat on the board.

"I'll call," he said and matched the bet.

Kettle rapped the table once and said, "Last card coming."

Kettle fingered the top card and turned it. "That's a four of hearts to Captain Hubbard, looking at a straight flush to the seven. And"—turning Animal's card—"a jack of spades for Mister Podberoski, a flush to the jack. Jack-high bets."

Animal kept his eyes off Hubbard, not even looking down at the jack that had just given him the flush. He took the washcloth and ran it over his face and arms and left it over the back of his neck. Cigar ashes fell into his lap, and he quickly brushed them away.

Looking into the face of a possible straight flush, he knew he had only one bet.

"Check once more to the bomber," he said in a strong voice.

"That's a check to you, Captain Hubbard," Kettle repeated.

The only sound in the hold came from the dull roar of the ship's engines and a creak here and there from the GIs moving around to get a better look. Hubbard waited. Animal waited. Kettle placed the deck on the table and sat back with his fingers joined in his lap.

Hubbard made the first move by leaning forward and looking straight into Animal's eye.

"I see you have approximately forty-five thousand dollars in your stack, is that right?"

"That's right," Animal said, his voice tighter now.

"Then that's my bet. Forty-five thousand dollars."

"Forty-five thousand to you, Mister Podberoski."

"I heard him the first time."

Animal spent the next few seconds counting out the money, pushing the bills out in front of him so that Hubbard could see him. Once he had it counted, he stacked the money and eased it over next to the ashtray.

Then he relit the cigar and spread his cards out in front of him . . . little things to keep his fingers busy while his brain did the work of trying to figure out whether Hubbard was lying or not.

He ran down the possibilities: he could call the forty-five grand and lose, which would mean the end; or fold and stay alive for the next hand; or call the bet and win, in which case his stake would be up around a hundred and seventy-five thousand. It was a hell of a position to be in, having a jack-high flush and worried to death that it wasn't enough.

Looking over at Hubbard didn't help because the guy was wearing the same poker face he always wore.

"What is it to me?" he asked, stalling.

"Forty-five thou," Kettle said.

"Right." He shifted the cigar to the other side of his mouth and unconsciously drummed his fingers on the table, trying to stay cool but knowing that staying cool didn't make any difference right now because it was all up to him. And then he got this funny feeling in his head that he wanted everything to stop dead and let him stay right where he was without doing a thing and take just as long as he damn well pleased to make up his mind. He didn't want to call, or raise, or do anything but stay put, which of course was impossible, but he thought it was a pretty funny thing to think about at the moment.

"All right," he said, taking a deep breath and sliding his hand over to the piles of cash. "I'll call."

Hubbard turned over his hole card and Animal looked into the stoic red face of the queen of hearts, but for a moment he just sat there, not realizing that he had lost. Finally, Hubbard broke the silence with, "Can you beat that?"

Animal never took his eyes off the queen.

"No, I can't," he said quietly.

The hold was as quiet as death and except for the gentle pitch and roll of the ship the only movement was Hubbard's as he dragged the money in.

"You still playing?" he asked Animal.

"Not hardly, Cap'n," he said, and then with a kind of half-amused grin on his face, added, "I knew I shouldna shaved."

Chapter Fourteen

AT EIGHT-THIRTY the next morning the radio operator received a transmission that was so unusual he asked to have it repeated. Then, unable to reach Chief Mate Murphy on the intercom, he left his station and headed for Murphy's quarters, where he found him sleeping.

"What's so goddamn important?" Murphy grumbled.

"This," the operator said, handing over the transmission.

Murphy read it, and read it again.

"This for real?"

"Twice," the operator said. "It came in twice."

"Okay, Flynn, go back to work. Let me know if anything else comes in."

Murphy scrambled into his clothes, left the room and headed for Number 4 hold. On the main deck he ran into Larry Kettle.

"Here." Murphy handed him the message. "Read this."

Kettle read it. Murphy saw the confusion on his face. "This can't be right," Kettle said.

"Flynn took the message twice. I've got to carry out the order."

Kettle handed the message back to him. "Something's wrong here, Murphy. You go on take care of business and I'll be up with the radio, to make sure."

"I'll be in Number Four getting some men."

"Gotcha."

Murphy hustled across the deck and dropped through Number 4 hatch. Inside the hold he scouted around for the sentries, rousted them out of the sack, and in a few minutes, carbines slung over their shoulders, they were following Murphy out of Number 4, back across the main deck and up the ladder leading to the officers' quarters.

They reached the top of the ladder and climbed down, Murphy pressing his finger to his lips for quiet, then crept slowly along the steel-riveted corridor, passing beneath the swaying overhead bulbs and halting just outside a doorway. Murphy motioned for them to unsling their weapons.

Stepping into the doorway, he said, "Captain Hubbard?"

Hubbard looked up from his book. "Yes, Mister Murphy, what is it?"

It was obvious to Hubbard, as he saw the armed guard moving in behind him, that it was no casual visit.

"I'm here to place you under arrest," Murphy told him.

"Arrest?"

"That's right," he said, handing him the radiogram. "This just came in."

The message read: PLACE UNDER ARREST HUBBARD EVAN A CAPT US ARMY STOP SERIAL NUMBER ONE FOUR SEVEN SEVEN NINE ZERO EIGHT ONE STOP FOR HOMICIDE RAF MAJOR STOP CASABLANCA FOUR SEPTEMBER THIS

YEAR STOP POSITIVE PRINT WEAPON ID HOLD FOR
CAPTURE.

The authorization came from a Military Police Detachment Major Haines at the Brooklyn Army Base.

"Know anything about that, Captain?"

Hubbard felt . . . no, not exactly shock . . . more like
rage, rage that he had just won the biggest poker game
of his life, and now it had been blown sky high because
of that sniveling little Major who wouldn't leave him
alone and had come back from the dead—from the dead,
goddamn it—to wipe away every one of his dreams. If
that bastard had been in front of him now, he would
have quite willingly blown his goddamn head off.

"Yes," he said to Murphy, "I know something about
it." He got off the bed and started dressing.

When one of the guards pulled out a set of handcuffs
Murphy ordered him to put it away, with a quick smile
to show Hubbard that he trusted him to come along
peaceably, officer to officer.

Murphy said they would have to take a back way
down to the brig because he didn't want any of the men
to see that he was under guard and start asking questions,
and in the middle of his explanation Murphy slipped in
the word "humiliating," which Hubbard could understand: it would be rather humiliating for everyone to
know that he had been thrown in the brig after winning
a half-million-dollar poker game. He thanked Murphy
for his consideration.

He could also tell that Murphy was dying of curiosity
by the way he kept saying what a shame it was that it
had to happen, and was there anything he could do to
make things more comfortable for him, and he was sure
there was probably some big mistake.

"*Is* there some mistake?" Murphy finally asked him
outside the cell.

"I'll take care of it, Mister Murphy."

"Well, fine. If there's anything I can do, just holler. Meanwhile, your money is tucked away in the safe, so . . ."

"I appreciate it."

There didn't seem to be anything else to say so Murphy opened the cell door and Hubbard walked inside.

Just after noon Animal was on his way down to sick bay to visit Augie and Santini when he heard a wild rumor that Evan Hubbard had been arrested and thrown in the brig. He changed course immediately and made straight for the brig. The news shocked the hell out of him. Hubbard *arrested?* For what? What the hell could Hubbard have done?

The sentry wouldn't tell him what Hubbard had done, nor would he let him inside.

"Hubbard!" Animal shouted. "You in there!"

"I'm here."

"I'll have to ask you to leave," the sentry told Animal.

"Fuck off. Get Murphy down here. I wanna talk to Hubbard."

"I'm afraid I can't—"

"Lissen asshole, pick up that horn and tell Murphy to get his ass down here. Otherwise, I'll put a fucking hole in your face. Move!"

The sentry edged away and called Murphy.

"Hang on, Cap'n," Animal shouted. "I'll be there in a minute."

The brig was like a clammy dungeon: even his breathing sounded metallic. It gave him the creeps. What also gave him the creeps was that Hubbard was locked up in the first place. And the reason it gave him the creeps was that it was just one more thing that shouldn't have happened. Just like Santini's system being stolen shouldn't have happened, or Charlie Buck going overboard, or Augie getting food poisoning and then Santini again with his mind snapped. When he thought about it he and Hubbard were the only survivors of the fucking trip across the Atlantic. That is, until now. Now he was the only survivor.

The sentry came back to tell him that Murphy would be down shortly.

"Thanks. Murph'll be here in a second, Cap'n!"

"Right!"

Animal sat down on the bottom rung of the ladder. He wondered, what with everything else going on, if somehow even the game had been set up to have Hubbard win. He didn't see how the hell that was possible, especially since Hubbard was now locked up.

He wished to hell Augie would get his throat cleared up so he could talk. But the poor fucker couldn't even move, much less say anything, at least that was the case early this morning when he checked in with him. He would go to sick bay right after seeing Hubbard to find out what Augie meant by having "figured it out."

The really weird thing about all this was the purpose behind it. That's what bugged him. The why. Why were all these things happening, and who was making them happen? And what did that person want?

Everything that had happened to Santini, Charlie, Augie and Hubbard *could* have been accidents—except for one thing. Poncho. Somebody killed his bird. That was the clincher. When Augie had talked about sabotage and all that shit, he'd been sure that it *was* all shit. But when he found Poncho . . .

Whoever was behind all these things had fucked up when he went after his bird, because it had made everything else so blatantly obvious. Not only was it a sick man Animal was dealing with, but somebody who wasn't that bright ... which in a way made him even more dangerous.

He heard bootsteps coming down the ladder and turned to find Murphy staring down at him.

"What's this all about, Podberoski?"

Animal stood.

"I wanna see Hubbard."

"He's off limits."

"Murphy, he's in jail. And even if he wasn't in jail, where the hell would he go? Have your asshole here keep a watch on me. I wanna see Hubbard, and if you don't let me see him I'll be up there on deck saying that you and your crew are trying to steal Hubbard's money by locking him up. How'd you like a mutiny on your hands?"

"Open the door," Murphy said to the sentry.

"Okay, Cap'n," Animal said, moving inside, "start talkin'."

Chapter Fifteen

SAM MURPHY guided the *John Logan* toward the thin dark line of the horizon forming off the starboard bow. In the wheelhouse with him was the radio operator, Flynn, another Irishman from Massachusetts, who'd been his radioman for four years and who shared with him a common sadness about this last voyage of the ship, for within a short time the ship would be turned into scrap. The two of them sat drinking coffee together, as they'd done hundreds of times before, talking about the old days when they'd sailed together with the first Libertys.

Murphy was looking out now through the wheelhouse window, down to the deck where the troops were gathering, waiting to catch their first glimpse of home. Even though this was his fourth time hauling troops across the Atlantic in the last eight months, he still felt a rash of goosebumps sweep over him when he saw the excitement on their faces.

Kettle tramped in, bleary-eyed and hunched over, and grunted hello on his way to the coffee pot, where he slugged down two cups and then joined Murphy by the window.

"I'll tell you one thing," he said, yawning. "I couldn't ever play poker for a living. One night with those guys was enough and I wasn't even playing."

"What *are* you going to do for a living, Kettle?" Murphy asked, already knowing the answer but liking to hear it anyway because it was exactly what he planned on doing himself.

"Nothin'. Not a goddamn thing. I'm gonna sit back on my ass and watch Kentucky for about a year. I'm so damn tired of being on water."

"I won a hundred bucks on Hubbard," Flynn said. "Who'd you bet on, Mister Kettle?"

"I didn't. Didn't think it was ethical."

Murphy thought that was funny. "*Ethical?* Will miracles never cease . . . When did this happen?"

"I'm not kiddin', running the game like I was, I didn't think it'd be right to play favorites . . . but what a life, playing poker for that kind of money. Sitting down with 'em for just one day I got more sense of what those fellas go through than the whole week I was standing up next to them at the table. But after Charlie Buck died, God rest his soul, I sorta figured on Hubbard. He was so damn cool I just figured he had to win."

Kettle gulped down the rest of the coffee. "It's too bad about this other thing."

"Yeah, I know," Murphy sighed. "Podberoski talked with Hubbard and told me he was in a lot of trouble."

"He did it, huh, knocked off the guy?"

"According to Podberoski, who also said there were extenuating circumstances."

"What kind of circumstances?"

"Hell if I know . . ."

Kettle took their cups over for a refill. "What do you think we oughta do about his money?"

"I thought about that and I figure the only thing we can do is leave it in the safe, put a guard on it, and wait to see what happens," Murphy said. "I'll know better when I hand him over to the MPs."

"All right," said Kettle, "I'll take care of it. But right now I have to check the cargo, see if those damn wrenches still work after the storm."

And with that he marched out, whistling an off-key version of "My Old Kentucky Home."

Animal had not slept. After losing the heartbreak hand, then visiting Hubbard in the clink and Epstein and Santini in sick bay, he was too pumped up to even try. Besides, he liked the way he felt, as if he'd gone beyond sleep into a kind of dopey dreamland where he felt unbelievably clean and slower-moving and slower-thinking, and clearer-thinking. It was like being drunk without the taste of booze.

Thinking back over the crossing it all seemed unreal to him, a dream of poker hands and being cramped in his chair, of rolling around in The Tomb down there as the ship tilted from one side to the other. He could have run over every big hand, card by card, bet by bet, if he'd wanted to, but he didn't. That was in the past. Poncho was in the past, too. It would have been great to show off the bird that saved his life. At least he had the newspaper clippings . . . Jesus, if he could have put his hands around the neck of the bastard who killed her, but . . . He thought about all the weird happenings—Poncho, of course, and Santini, Charlie Buck, Augie, Hubbard taking the last hand. He knew the trip across would be stamped in his brain forever.

And now he had problems waiting for him out there ... money ... Mildred and her kids ... the headache of finding a job and a place to live ... but all that could wait for a minute. He had stepped onto the bridge now to see what everyone else had come to see, out there in the clear, late afternoon sun. Land. Long Island.

When he had told Santini that he could hardly remember what home was like, he hadn't been kidding. Six years away could do that. The only connection he'd had was by letter, but those didn't come too often because his family never did like to write. He'd read other guys' letters, some of them like stories, but they meant home to somebody else. Every once in a while, overseas replacements would come into the battalion but they were so shocked by everything going on that they never said very much. The movies helped. He could see what people were wearing and listen to the new tunes, but every one of them was like a gingerbread land that didn't exist except in some guy's mind in Hollywood. They were fun, though. They made him laugh.

So he really didn't know, after six years, what to expect. It was funny, he'd spent twenty-eight years in the same Brooklyn neighborhood and now, except for a few things here and there, most of it was a blur. He even worried about not recognizing his family, it was that bad. He had a couple of pictures ... but they were about six years old, too. ...

His plan had been to be wide awake and looking like a million bucks when the ship docked, but that was out of the question after last night ... Jeez, you don't suppose they wouldn't recognize *him* either, do you? After all, he was older, and looked it. The pudgy baby face had inherited a few trenchlines around the nose and eyes:

character lines was the word his mother would use. Wearing a helmet all the time had driven his hairline back a couple of inches, and he had spotted those little gray mothers sprouting around his ears . . .

He remembered what his best buddy, the late Jerry Crews, had said to him about going home. It was a different world, he'd said, you won't recognize it when you get there. A man who's been in war has to understand that nothing in civilian life could ever match the day-by-day, life-on-the-line excitement of combat. In order to stay sane, that man would have to find some other kind of excitement to keep him busy . . . Animal wondered what that would be . . .

And then all those thoughts were wiped from his mind when he saw the south shore of Long Island on the right, and up ahead, and then around the bend, the Manhattan skyline, at which point the memories started flooding back and the hair stood up on his arms; and he sensed how everything, the houses and the trees and even the smell of the place, was different, like an old neighborhood you went back to that might have changed over the years but never lost the special feeling you have for it.

Animal didn't really know what to expect or how he'd act or even if he would be happy after the initial shock of coming home wore off. He *did* know, however, as the tug came out to meet the ship, that somewhere among the crowd of people waiting on the dock was his family, and that was enough for now.

Hauling his B-bag on his shoulder, Animal climbed down the ladder to the deck and moved with the flow of troops along the starboard railing as the *John Logan* made its final maneuver in the murky Hudson and steered into Slip 42.

The crowd on the dock wasn't that large, most of the

troops lived a long way from New York and they'd have to be discharged first and get their trip tickets home. Besides, the way the Army ran things, most of the soldiers hadn't really believed they were going home till they were on the ship and heading out to sea—so how could they have written that they'd be arriving on such and such a date in such and such a ship? Across the deck, Animal caught sight of Augie and Santini being prepared by medical aides for off-loading on the port side.

Down a few bodies from Animal, a couple of GIs spotted relatives and started dancing around and shouting and nearly falling over the rail. Soldiers around him were boasting about the first thing they were going to do when they hit the town: "I'm telling you, boy, I'm gonna get one hell of a drunk on." "Shit, that might be all right for you, but *I* am heading for the sweetest little piece of ass you ever—"

Animal felt a tap on his shoulder and turned around to find Larry Kettle's freckled face smiling up at him.

"Like to say good-bye to you, Mister Podberoski," he said, shaking Animal's hand. "It was a real pleasure meetin' you and being a part of the game and all."

Animal slapped him hard on the back, and Kettle winced. "Well, thank you, Kettle. You treated us real good and we all appreciate it. Best of luck to you."

"Gotta get on down through Customs now, check the shore cargo and—"

"Me, too? I have to go through Customs?"

"No, no." Kettle chuckled. "Just the crew. You fellas can take all the cameras and jewels you want, free as a bird. Take care now."

"You bet." Free as a bird.

Animal stayed at the railing for a few more minutes, searching the crowd, when suddenly there she was, bigger than ever, her wide, round, open face beaming up at him, plowing through the crowd, batting people out of her way, screaming at the top of her lungs: "Edwaaaard!" His mother, and behind her, in the huge wedge she opened, were the rest of them: his father, brothers and sisters, Mildred and her two kids who were soon going to be his two kids, aunts and uncles and cousins, even Gramma Bette who must be over eighty by this time. Could he handle all this, all at once?

The gangplank was lowered and a moment later more than two hundred soldiers swarmed down toward the dock—which meant nothing to Animal's mother who charged right up through them.

Animal yelled out, "Ma! Wait! I'll be right there. Ma! Don't!" But she did, and beautifully, driving troops against the handrails, bulldozing through them like a fullback. She was shouted at, cursed at, pushed at, but no one tried to stop her.

Animal couldn't believe it: a sixty-year-old woman, his own mother, stampeding up at him like this. As her face appeared and disappeared in the sea of heads, he saw the fierceness on her, her eyes nearly closed and a snarl on her lips, and he watched her great white arms, like oars, pulling her way up.

"Edwaaaaaard!"

And then a moment later they stood facing each other. Nearly out of breath and faint, she held onto the railing for a second, to catch her breath, and then with eyes filling with tears of joy, she whispered, almost in disbelief, "Edward?"

"Hello, Ma," he said and thundered into her arms.

The slim, erect figure of Major Peter Tat waited just beyond the crowd's perimeter. His uniform was brand-new, requisitioned especially for this occasion, and he'd gone to Lawrence at the Waldorf to have his hair and mustache clipped and trimmed. Behind him parked against the curb was a staff car loaned to him by General Thorson, with a driver and telephone and two ice buckets filled with the best champagne he could find.

So certain was he that Charlie had won the game that he had made reservations at Small's Paradise up in Harlem, along with two of Manhattan's premier ladies of the night, reserved adjoining suites at the Plaza, and picked out a gold watch for the kid, with an inscription that read: *Poker ain't gambling. Tat. 9/14/45,* from something Charlie once said to him about horse bettors and casino players being gamblers. Great poker players never gambled, they *knew*.

So Tat waited while the GIs moved down the gangplank and fell into formation over by the trucks, thinking about how great the kid was and what a future he had at the table, and how he would manage him the best way he knew, and together they'd build an empire.

Hell, he thought, the publicity alone from winning a half-million-dollar game was enough to put them in the big leagues forever.

Larry Kettle waited by the loading dock for the wide, interminable arc of the cargo boom to swing the platform over the side and drop it gently into place.

"All right, fellas," he said to his crew members, "that crate goes into the truck on the left, and that into the one on the right. Put that in the jeep."

It took Kettle twenty minutes to check off the crates against his voucher and then he told everybody to load up, gave the truck drivers the address of the warehouse and then climbed into the jeep.

"Okay," he said to the driver, "let's go."

"Captain Hubbard, you ready?"

Murphy's face filled the hole in the cell door.

"Yeah." Hubbard grabbed his jacket and, slinging it over his shoulder, walked through the door.

"Hope you don't mind, Captain, but . . ." Murphy said, motioning for the guard to put handcuffs on, ". . . it's SOP."

"I wouldn't have it any other way," Hubbard said, holding his hands behind his back.

As they marched through the corridors leading away from the brig, Hubbard felt surprisingly calm; the last few hours cooped in the cell had given him the time he needed to put himself in the right frame of mind. He had reached a decision: he would stand trial without calling for his father's help. When he learned of his predicament, the General would undoubtedly truck out all his influence and favors due to get his son off, but Hubbard would resist . . . and not because he was being noble.

The trial would bring a great deal of publicity, of that he was sure, and he could see the headlines now: SON REFUSES FATHER'S HELP, SAYS JUSTICE WILL WIN OUT. It sounded very good—especially since he knew all the while his father would be cranking up wheels behind the scenes anyway.

He was not worried about the death itself: it was self-defense after all. His only real crime was leaving the scene, which the prosecution would no doubt play up as much as it could. To say that he suddenly panicked would not do, nor that he had been rushing off to play in a half-million-dollar poker game. He *could* say, of course, that after the Major fell, he looked up and saw the RAF flyers streaming out of the bar and felt that his life was in danger, and that once he got back to the safety of the States, he had planned on turning himself in. Would the Military Tribunal believe him? If he could bluff men like Podberoski and Epstein at the poker table, why not a court-martial board?

Major Tat felt that he had waited long enough. The last of the troops had departed the ship and now stood in formation waiting to be loaded on deuce-and-a-halfs to be taken to the center for discharge. He had seen one of the players—Podberoski—bound down the gangplank into his mother's arms, but instead of trying to push through the crowd himself, Tat decided to wait for his boy. But his boy had not shown. Was something wrong? Was Charlie waiting for the last possible minute to surprise him, perhaps? The last possible minute had passed; it was starting to get dark.

With a final look around, Tat headed for the gangplank and started up, reaching the deck and moving toward the huge uptake valves where he remembered accommodations were housed. Just then he spotted Chief Mate Murphy climbing down from the bridge, with another of the players, Hubbard, who seemed to be . . . Tat couldn't make out exactly what—handcuffed?

"Mister Murphy!" he called out and strode up to him.

Hubbard *was* handcuffed and the two sentries had their weapons raised.

"Captain Hubbard," Tat said, nodding to him.

"Afternoon, sir."

To Murphy, Tat said, "I'm looking for Charlie Buck, have you seen him?"

From the look on Murphy's face, Tat could tell that something was wrong.

"I don't quite know how to tell you this, Major, but—"

"—but? But what! Is Charlie all right?"

"No, sir. He's dead. Died at sea, an honorable death. He went overboard in a storm."

Tat looked as if he didn't hear him, at least didn't *want*

to hear him, by the crooked smile that jerked up on his lips, but there was no mistaking the burst of squint-eyed shock on his face.

"You are joking . . . aren't you?"

"I told you, Major, he's dead."

Tat looked at Hubbard for confirmation, and got it.

"Oh, my God." Tat hung onto the railing as dizziness took hold of him.

He happened to be blocking their progress by standing at the foot of the ladder, so Murphy said, "We said a mass for a repose of his soul, Major. Would you mind letting us pass, sir, so I can get along here."

"Overboard?" Tat said in a whisper.

"That's right, sir."

"Was he ahead?"

"Beg pardon?"

"Was Charlie ahead when he died? Was he winning?"

"Yes, he was, far as I know. Ask Captain Hubbard here. He was the big winner."

"Charlie had a hundred and forty-five thousand at the time he died, Major," Hubbard told him.

"Yes? Where's his money?"

"All the money's in the ship's safe," said Murphy, "ready for disposition. If you'll go up to the wheelhouse, Major, I'll take care of this business and meet you there in a few minutes."

"Yes." Tat backed away allowing them to pass, then pointed to Hubbard's handcuffs and said vaguely, "What's all this?"

"Nothing that concerns you, Major. Go on up to the wheelhouse; I'll be along shortly."

Murphy stood with Hubbard and the sentries at the foot of the gangplank for twenty minutes, wondering why in hell the MP detachment was late—it should have been here an hour ago. The darkness had spread over the city so that the only light came from a few streetlamps near the warehouse district and a smattering of autos rumbling up the West Side Highway.

Murphy tried striking up a conversation with Hubbard, but the Captain's one-line replies discouraged anything further, so Murphy waited another ten minutes and then told the sentries to keep their eyes on Hubbard while he went up to the radio.

Major Tat was a nervous wreck by the time Murphy returned to the wheelhouse.

"Well?" Tat said, his voice filled with tension.

"The MPs haven't shown. I'll have to call the Base."

He got hold of the Brooklyn Army Base operator who told him that everyone had gone home for the evening.

"Give me the MP detachment," Murphy told him. "This is top priority."

The operator switched him to the orderly room, where the OD came on the line. Murphy explained the situation and the officer was back a minute later with a reply.

"Sorry, Mister Murphy, but we have no information on that."

"What about the detachment that's supposed to be here to get Hubbard?"

"There's nothing about a detachment. There's nothing about an Evan Hubbard."

"Just a minute." Murphy took time to organize his thoughts. "I have a message here in front of me that came over my radio, ordering me to arrest Captain Evan Hubbard, for homicide, for killing an RAF major in Casablanca, September four. One of your officers sent it, a Major Haines."

"Sorry, sir, but we have no Major Haines in the MP Detachment."

Murphy repeated it. "Then check the *rest* of the Base,

would you—Major Richard *Haines*."

He heard the officer rustle through papers. "No such person," the OD said.

"H. . .A. . .I. . .N. . .E. . .S. Haines, Richard."

"Don't have him. And this roster came out just yesterday."

"You *are* the MP Detachment at the Brooklyn Army Base?"

"Yes, sir."

"Jesus, Mary and Joseph," Murphy muttered. "What the hell's going on here."

"Well," the officer said, trying to help, "you might have gotten the message wrong."

"Sure looks that way," Murphy said and broke communication. Looking up at Tat, he added, "You know anything about this, Major?"

"Me? All I know is that Charlie is dead and there's a hundred and forty-five thousand dollars of his—and my —money in your safe. May I see it now?"

"All right."

It was a short walk to the safe, where they found Kettle's two guards. Out of the others' view, Murphy worked the dial and opened the safe.

"Murphy?" Major Tat said after waiting a good ten seconds. "Murphy?"

Tat stepped up behind him and looked into the safe. Murphy slowly turned around to Tat and said in a low whisper, "It's empty."

"What do you mean, empty?"

"Gone. All the money's gone. Charlie Buck's and Hubbard's as well. Gone."

Murphy turned on the guards, "Has anyone been up here? Has anyone opened the safe?"

"No, sir," one of them said. "Nobody but Mister Kettle."

Chapter Sixteen

LARRY KETTLE did not follow the trucks to the ware-
houses. Instead he was driven north along the Hudson
into Westchester County, to a small airfield outside of
White Plains, where the driver pulled up and flashed his
headlights. Off in the distance, Kettle saw the answering
light and the driver continued along the blacktop road,
passing Convairs and other military planes that in the
darkness looked like old surplus craft that had probably
been stored here for repairs or scrap.

The jeep drove to the very end of the field and made
a sharp right, stopping at a DC-4 with its engines going.
Kettle and the driver got out and went to the rear of the
jeep, hefted a crate to their shoulders and carried it to the
rear baggage compartment, where a set of hands dropped
down to help them lift the crate inside. The door closed
and the two of them walked around to the steps that had
been dropped for them.

Entering the craft, the driver led Kettle through the

darkness to a seat and told him he would find a seat belt and would he please strap himself in. He felt the driver drop into the next seat and then listened to the engines rev and the plane begin to turn and move forward into position for take-off.

Not a word had been spoken since the driver had greeted him at the dock area in what had sounded like a Spanish accent. Kettle had thought it was all a little bit too cloak-and-dagger, but since the driver probably couldn't speak English anyway, he had settled back for the ride.

The take-off was as smooth as possible, considering the shape the strip was in—gutted-out tar with potholes all over. Kettle felt the wheels leave the ground and the landing gear clank up into the belly and the plane soar until his ears started to pop.

The single light in the plane was small and red, up front toward the cockpit. Out through the window he could see what he presumed were the lights of Manhattan and a smattering of suburban homes, and then nothing but pitch blackness.

"You mind if I smoke?" he asked the driver.

"Not at all," a voice answered, but it wasn't the driver's because the driver was on his left. The response had come from his right, and was followed by the striking of a match.

As the flame diminished, Kettle found himself looking into the white-mustachioed countenance of Sir Bertram Foote.

"Hello, Mr. Kettle," Bertram smiled. "Welcome aboard."

Kettle recovered after a second and said, "Sir Bertram, how yuh doing?"

"Marvelously well." Bertram turned to his right and said, "Flip the light on, darling, would you?"

When the light came on, Kettle saw the dark, beautiful face of Catherine de Conde.

"Hello, Mister Kettle," she said, her French accent lilting her words. "Would you care for something to drink?"

"Miss De Conde," Kettle said, nodding to her. "Bourbon on the rocks."

"Baez . . ." Kettle's driver unstrapped his seat belt and moved down the aisle toward the front. "I trust you both had an uneventful journey from the city," Catherine said.

"Yes, ma'am. Uneventful, that's the right word."

"Splendid."

"The crate you bought with you," Bertram said, "the money's in it?"

"Yes, sir."

"All of it?"

"Half a million dollars, yessir, every last cent of it."

Baez appeared with a tray of drinks which he placed in the aisle between them. Kettle watched him as he handed out the drinks and napkins and the plate of small sandwiches: somehow he didn't look as menacing as he had in the jeep.

"You might be interested in knowing, Mister Kettle," Bertram said in a chatty, offhanded way, "that Baez here was instrumental in our little enterprise, weren't you, Baez?"

"Yes, indeed, and it was great fun," Baez replied with a British inflection that surprised Kettle.

"Baez gave a virtuoso performance," Bertram went on, "as the RAF Major in Casablanca that Captain Hubbard murdered."

"You mean, Hubbard didn't—"

"No, no, but he *believed* he did and consequently gave no resistance when he was placed under arrest, true?"

"He went along peaceful as hell," Kettle said in admiration. "That's just perfect, Sir Bertram, damn!"

"Thank you. It was Catherine's idea. Baez is her manservant."

"The very best," Catherine added. "He's been with me longer than I've known Bert. But tell me, Mister Kettle, how did you manage to execute so perfectly your end of the bargain?"

Kettle held up his glass. "Could I have another one of these?"

"Excuse me," Baez said and leaned across his body to the lower shelf of the tray and pulled out the bottle of bourbon and some ice.

Kettle explained how he had sneaked in and stolen Santini's system, which had been like God to the guy, and how after that Santini had gone off the deep end. "He probably would have anyway, the way things were going, but with the system gone he did it faster." Then he said he had let some mayonnaise spoil and fed it to Augie Epstein and that Epstein deserved it anyway for discovering the two sides of beef Kettle had stored away.

"Epstein was also asking a lot of questions," Kettle said, "so I planned to keep feeding him the spoiled food so he wouldn't talk, except that when the ship's surgeon pumped Epstein's stomach he put the tube down his windpipe instead of his esophagus and ruined his vocal cords for a couple of days. What a break! So I was safe there."

Podberoski had been the toughest one of all: Kettle had tried throwing him off by making sure his pet canary met with an accident, but that hadn't seemed to faze him all that much, so as a final recourse, he crawled among the pipe casings above his room and banged on the pipes all night long, hoping that when Podberoski played the final day against Hubbard, he would be too tired to keep his concentration up.

"Was he?" Catherine asked.

"He could hardly keep his eyes open. I can't be absolutely sure that's what did him in—but the important thing is he *did* lose."

"Yes," Bertram said, "but what if he had started winning?"

"Oh, I had alternative plans all the way down the line, for *all* the players. Getting them sick like Epstein was always a possibility, and of course, if worse came to worse, I could've injured them in their sleep, which I really didn't want to do, 'cause that would have been too obvious. I had to make everything *look* right, at least so they didn't feel their lives were in danger."

"Yes, I can see that," Bertram agreed.

"When you told me that Hubbard had to win, no matter what, I promised you I'd get the job done—no matter what. Which I did."

"Yes indeed," Bertram said, "and beautifully."

There was a slight pause before Catherine asked, "You've said nothing of the young man, Charlie Buck. What method did you use to eliminate him?"

Kettle slugged down the rest of his drink and poured another.

"Fell overboard," he said.

"Fell overboard?"

"Yes, ma'am, we had this storm and twenty-four men went overboard, including Charlie Buck. That's what happened to him."

"That's terrible!" Catherine said.

"Yes'm, I liked Charlie, too, really did," Kettle replied, avoiding her gaze.

It was obvious there was more to it than that, but

Bertram and Catherine decided not to pursue it.

"Well then," Sir Bertram said, "you've performed magnificently, Mister Kettle—as we all have, I must say."

"Hear, hear!" Catherine raised her glass. "To our success, all our success, and good fortune."

They toasted one another, and Bertram said, "How did you manage to get the money off the ship by the way? Wasn't stuffing it in a crate rather risky?"

"That's the best part, Sir Bertram," Kettle told him. "I had to go through Customs myself, and of course the crates were all inspected. Those sides of beef I told you about—I let the players have one of them, but the other one"—he paused for a moment with pride of authorship —"the second one I hollowed out, you know, in between the ribs there, and stuck the money in a plastic bag up inside, real snug-like, and then I stitched it up again. To tell you the truth, Epstein gave me the idea when he wanted the meat for himself. Neat, huh?" Kettle beamed.

"As a pin, Mister Kettle." Bertram smiled. "As a pin."

Their plan was to make a fuel stop south of Miami and then continue on for three hundred miles to the southeast, to Cat Island, a member of the Bahamas group and a British Protectorate, where an old chum of Bertram's had a villa. After a week or so in the sun to rest up—and just to make sure no one was following them— they would head for Catherine's Casa de Las Aguilas on the Gibraltar Strait.

From the air, the island had the shape of a pistol without the trigger mechanism, and at first looked barren, desolate. None of them had ever been here before—had never heard of it, in fact—but from what Bertram's chum had told him, Cat Island was about fifty miles long and two miles wide at its widest point. The runway was dirt, but long enough to handle a DC-4 and, not coincidentally, ended just a hundred meters from the villa's front steps.

As the pilot made a pass over the strip, however, to see what he had to contend with, they noticed that part of the island was not barren at all, but lush with foliage and bordered by a white undulating beach, with the clearest water any of them had ever seen. *This* was more like it.

After the plane had landed and they had climbed down into breezy eighty-degree sunshine, Catherine ordered Baez and the pilot to bring their bags and the provisions they had bought in Florida—and the crate— to the house. When they stepped inside, they smiled with pleasure. It was obvious that Bertram's friend had spent a fortune importing the tile, the marble, the redwood pillars and ceilings, porcelain and stained glass that adorned the place, and it was also apparent that someone on the island kept the house up when he was away. Fresh linen covered the beds, water lapped in the pool, and down the hill flower beds bloomed in a multitude of colors.

"A week might turn into a month or more, dear," Bertram said to Catherine, who was busy on an inspection tour, identifying the origin of this tapestry and the value of that.

"And you should see his library!" she called from the next room.

Kettle sauntered out to test the pool water, and promptly ripped off his uniform and jumped in.

After Baez and the pilot finished bringing in the gear, Bertram extracted a bottle of champagne from one of the cases and called for everyone to join him. He made a note to repay his chum's hospitality in some extravagant way: this "cottage on the water," as the fellow had called it, was a damn paradise.

They drank champagne for the next half hour or so until Bertram could wait no longer. He asked Baez to shove Kettle's crate over so they all could feast their eyes on their half-million-dollar "booty."

"Mister Kettle," Bertram said with one foot on the crate, "would you do the honors?"

"Be happy to."

Baez went out back somewhere and returned with a crowbar, which Kettle used to pry open the boards.

"I'll need a sharp knife."

Baez was back with one in no time.

Kettle got down on his knees and started cutting slowly through the stitches. Halfway through he yanked a piece of the plastic bag out to show everyone, for which he received a round of applause, then, the stitches cut in two, he reached inside and began carefully pulling it out into the open. He thought back to early that morning, just after Hubbard's arrest, when he'd carried the money down and begun methodically hollowing out the inside of the beef and stuffing the money in, and then he'd had it taken to the hold for off-loading. Oh, this was sweet, he thought, pulling at the bag . . . here he'd been bowing and scraping to those fuckers all trip, doing this for them, doing that for them, and now look who had come out the winner in the end . . .

His excitement grew as he gave the bag a final tug and pulled it free of the meat, then with the knife, sliced through the plastic, exposing the cardboard box in which he had placed the money.

"*Et voilà,* as the French say!" he announced, winking at Catherine, looking up and seeing their faces relax and at the same time sparkle with anticipation. Sir Bertram leaned forward, as did Catherine.

Kettle proceeded to rip the tape from the box cover, removed the lid, and—what the hell?

He jumped back, unable to—cans. There were *cans* of *food* inside ... twenty of them, maybe thirty. He reached inside and frantically rummaged through the cans, all the way to the bottom. Nothing. There was no money.

"It's ... not here," he muttered. "Not *here*."

"What's that?" he heard Sir Bertram say.

"Not here. The money's not here."

There was suddenly a lot of activity in the room. Catherine sprang across the floor and poked her head inside the box, then, after a long moment, slowly straightened up.

"He's right," she said, her face like stone. "There's no money."

What they found instead was written on a piece of paper stuck between the cans—a letter.

Dear Kettle:

Surprise! You sonofabitch. You almost pulled it off, didn't you? You and that terrific couple, Sir Bertram and Catherine the Great, who had to be in on it because you're too goddamn stupid to have pulled it off by yourself. They picked you because you were the right man in the right place, right? Well, you sure made some wrong moves. Hiding the money in the beef ... clever, Mister Kettle, but not really. You couldn't carry the money off the boat with you because of Customs, right? So you had to haul it off in the cargo. Podberoski spent an hour going through the crates in the hold before he spotted the beef.

And you know when Podberoski made the switch? When you were making your final rounds, Kettle. Let that be a lesson to you: never establish patterns when you're a thief.

I've had your number for two days, and, yeah, I can talk now, just barely. I knew you engineered all those sick things you did because you were the only one

whose time I couldn't account for. And the bird...
that was too much. You blew it, and you, too, Bertie
and Cathy, you blew it too. Bertie, what a bad reflection
you are on the House of Commons!
Next time you try to pull something like this make sure
you know who you're up against. Toodaloo, you
fuckers, see you in Hell.

                    (Signed)
                    Augie Epstein
                    Edward "Animal" Podberoski

Epilogue

THOUGH THE POKER GAME ITSELF had not been rigged, the conditions had been, and so it was agreed upon by the players to divide the half million dollars equally, each retrieving his initial $100,000 investment.

MR. AND MRS. ROBERT BUCK, of Miles City, Montana, received their late son's share.

MAJOR PETER TAT retired from the U.S. Army as a Colonel in 1955, and is now employed by International Business Machines.

EVAN HUBBARD IV made his living as a professional card player for the next twelve years, until May, 1957, when he learned that his father, Major General Evan Hubbard III (U.S.A. Ret.), had drowned in a boating accident, at which time he returned to Mirabelle, the family estate, where he now resides with his mother.

MICHELANGELO SANTINI spent seventeen years in a private sanitarium, at the Army's expense. He now resides in Geneva, Switzerland, employed as a gardener in Parc de la Grange.

CHIEF MATE SAM MURPHY operates a tour-boat service in the Netherlands Antilles.

AUGIE EPSTEIN returned to Chicago and invested in a number of small businesses which turned an excellent profit, so that by 1958 he had made his first million.

EDWARD "ANIMAL" PODBEROSKI married Mildred Memory and is presently owner of a chain of retail furniture stores in Brooklyn, New York.

SIR BERTRAM FOOTE was defeated for reelection in 1948, and soon after retired to his country home in Essex, where at age sixty-five he passed away.

LARRY KETTLE's whereabouts since 1945 are not known.

CATHERINE DE CONDE, age seventy-three, resides in Gibraltar, at the Bristol on Cathedral Square. One of her favorite stories concerns the biggest poker game in all of World War II, held aboard the Liberty ship *John Logan,* and how she managed to walk away with half a million dollars.

A Poker Hand

A Poker hand consists of five cards. The value of a hand depends on whether it contains one of the following combinations:

Straight flush, the highest possible hand: all five cards of the same suit and in sequence, such as the 6, 7, 8, 9 and 10 of diamonds. The highest-ranking straight flush is the A, K, Q, J and 10 of one suit, called a *royal flush.*

Four of a kind rank next under a straight flush; for instance, four aces or four sixes. It does not matter what the fifth, unmatched card is.

A *full house* is three cards of one rank and two cards of another rank, such as 8-8-8-4-4, and ranks next under four of a kind.

A *flush* is five cards of the same suit, but not all in sequence, and ranks below a full house.

A *straight* is five cards in sequence, but not all of the same suit. It loses to a flush or higher hand, but beats anything else.

Three of a kind rank next under a straight.

Two pairs, as Q-Q-7-7-4, rank under three of a kind.

One pair beats any hand containing no pair but none of the high-ranking combinations named above.

And below the rank of hands containing one pair are all the no-pair hands, which are rated by the highest card they contain, so that an ace-high hand will beat a king-high hand, and so on.